THE GUARDIANS

Allie Byrons

Jane Alexandra Publishing

Copyright © 2024 Allie Byrons

Cover design © Jane Alexandra Publishing 2024

First published in Great Britain in 2024 by Jane Alexandra Publishing
www.janealexandrareads.com

The right of Allie Byrons to be identified as the author of this work have been asserted in accordance with the Copyright, Designs and Patents Act of 1988

All rights reserved. No part of this publication may be reproduced, stored in a retrieval system, or transmitted in any form or by any means, electronic, mechanical, photocopying, recording, or otherwise, without the prior permission of both the copyright owner and the above publisher of this book.

All the characters in this book are fictitious, and any resemblance to actual persons, living or dead, is purely coincidental.

CONTENTS

Title Page
Copyright
1.   1
2.   16
3.   30
4.   37
5.   53
6.   69
7.   82
8.   96
9.   109
10.   121
11.   140
About The Author   147

1.

I have never fallen into the trap of defining myself by the men in my life, so it is hard for me to concede the hold Tim had over me. I have tried to lay some of the blame on my parents (though they would have none of that): their relationship was always warm, easy and mutually supportive, so I grew up unpractised in the art or science of conflict and how to deal with it. Some of it may be because of Geoff. Oh, not Geoff himself – he is surely blameless in all that happened – but he and Tim could not have been more different if they had been designed for the purpose, so being sucked in by Tim was a reaction to the becalming influence of Geoff. They were opposites in every way: where Geoff was awkward, gawky even, Tim was agile and dynamic; while Geoff was laid back to the point of horizontality, Tim was into everything, passionate and opinionated; Geoff was sloppy, untidy, beyond casual, while Tim was always pristine and organised; they even looked so unalike they might almost have been different species – Tim as dark as Geoff was fair, Tim stocky where Geoff was rangy, Tim undeniably attractive, Geoff well, (sorry, Geoff) ordinary and unassuming. Now, I know I'm not stupid, and the fact that I can drive a car, do the ironing, negotiate life in general without inflicting self-injury tells me that I am capable of learning. And I have a good degree. OK, it's a fairly pointless subject for all but the rarest of careers – history – but maybe it demonstrates that my brain can operate at a certain level of competence, which is, after all, the purpose of most such qualifications. I can certainly absorb facts - I am known by friends and colleagues for my elephantine memory, and can recite the dates of great battles, not to mention Premier league statistics, with ease. I am also analytical and consciously self-aware, so where does this apparent blind spot about life-partners come from?

I met Geoff at university. It's a cliché, I know, but we were in all the same classes and tutor groups and bonded over all-nighters and our love of real ales. Many was the weekend we would abandon a dreary essay to head off in Geoff's rusting old Ford in search of a satisfying pint of something with a quirky name. We even had a little local brewery within walking distance of the college, where we became such frequent visitors that they put us on their mailing list for tasting sessions and artisan ale events. Not daft, these young brewers – they knew that proximity would ensure they had a constant stream of thirsty young customers amongst the alumni, and they kept the prices reassuringly low so their 'tasting room' (pub) was always full of both students and staff. And we could never choose a lasting favourite; we nearly settled on 'Drayman's Knob' (syrupy and bitter at the same time), until we found 'Cattleford Best' (a hint of fruit in hay). Then the brewery created the smoky 'Rurality' and we were back to having to try them all to confirm our favourites!

The arrogance of youth even found us sharing the condemnation of most of our tutors as 'out of touch', 'boring', or, most childish and baseless of all - 'picking on me', so it's a wonder we actually managed to complete our degrees between all the beer and affected disenchantment while we grew up. But we did, with varying success, and both had decent jobs 'with prospects' by the time we came back to swan about in black robes and silly hats and be handed a fake scroll by the Chancellor. Mind you, I don't think Geoff ever quite forgave me for getting a First when he had to settle for a Desmond.

That day we all went back for conferment was as much about catching up and showing off our new lives as it was

about receiving our qualifications. We were one of only three couples whose relationship, forged so strongly in the mutuality and familiarity of academic drudgery, had survived beyond the claustrophobic squalor of our three years in digs and halls. Naturally, the day would not have been complete without a final evening back in the tasting room at Nettles Bros, and we were not the only ones who began the next day with a fearsome hangover and more than a little embarrassment: Ted Sharma had actually dropped his trousers (and he wasn't wearing underwear!); Chris and Noelle's always volatile relationship finally bit the dust in a drunken and very public row about who was more pissed (I'm sure it mattered to them at the time); Marianne, who had gone straight back after uni to her childhood sweetheart at home, was sick in her own (thankfully cheap) handbag. There was much comment on who was doing what:
'Flipping burgers isn't a waste of an engineering degree, it's an opportunity', from Arthur, the MacDonald's king;
'Well, I'll be looking for a partnership in a couple of years' – sad, hopeful office junior and would-be silk Jaime;
'Just as well my dad owns the company,' chirruped Lorraine, the vacuous waste of space who had cheated her way to a scraped third with a great deal of help from a shady essay-writing website. Throughout the self-conscious jollity Geoff and I sat in judgement over them all, too smug in knowing that we were already beyond these children; we were grown-ups now, with a neat flat that we pretentiously re-branded as an 'apartment', fledgling careers, a smart car each, a wardrobe full of 'professional' clothes, a future.
Even when challenged by a distinctly bleary-eyed Raza – 'So when are you two getting married then?' we stayed self-contained and didn't commit ourselves beyond laughing at him (he thought we were laughing *with* him) but neither of us could imagine life without the other now, so we assumed our future along with everyone else.

That was the evening when I picked up the first inklings of how potentially one-sided and possibly unhealthy our relationship was, and it was a chance comment from Marianne that came back to me weeks later when it was all over. We had been talking nostalgically about the hobbies we had all embraced as students, about how none of us had the time any more for playing sports, or going to the gym, or even reading for pleasure – that had gone by the wayside when we were all too absorbed in getting through the tomes we had to digest for our courses, and none of us had time to get back into the habit of the frivolous side of life. Marianne differed from us all, however, and told us in (mostly redundant) detail about her sparkling career in local amateur dramatics,

'It's a bit of a commitment, two evenings a week, then time for learning all the lines, plus extra rehearsals at weekends sometimes. And the week of the show is frantic,' she twittered, clearly loving every minute of it, 'but you have to do the things you enjoy, don't you, not just work, work, work, or you'd shrivel up,' she finished. I didn't know whether to be envious or disparaging, but, before I could conjure either response Raza chipped in,

'And doesn't the sainted Harry mind his little woman being out all the time?' There was a bit of an intake of breath all around the table at his ludicrous sexism, but before I could voice what we were all thinking—something along the lines of 'who are you calling a 'little woman'?—Marianne put a full stop to the thread with,

'Mind? Why would he mind? I don't have to justify myself to him or anybody else.'

That launched the conversation firmly into a raucous and entirely flippant battle of the sexes, with Raza and Ted bemoaning the erosion of men's dominance in the world, and the women in the group defending their equal rights.

Apart from me, that is. I relapsed into thoughtful silence. Marianne's throwaway remark had made me think, just for a moment: I justified myself to Geoff often, making sure he knew where I was, checking with him before making arrangements with other people, apologising for personal failure, giving him a

time I would be home, and sticking to it scrupulously. Why did I do that? Did he expect it somehow, or was it coming from me? Was I unconsciously treating him as my younger self had my father? Was it from respect or deference, my own need to please other people, or his subliminal control? And did he always treat me with reciprocal courtesy? Finally, tired, I suppose, of my withdrawal from the conversation, Geoff nudged me, nearly spilling the pint I had been nursing untouched since my retreat,
'What's up with you, you miserable cow? You haven't said a word for hours. Drink up.'
I knew immediately that he was teasing, and I had never been offended by his use of mildly abusive epithets born of familiarity, but briefly I found myself wanting to question our interaction, to test my embryonic theory. I sensed immediately, however, that now was not the moment to raise it with him: not only were we in a large group, and I was far too British to 'wash my dirty linen in public', as my mum would have reminded me, but I knew I was drunk and therefore hardly thinking clearly. I was still aware enough to not trust what might have come out of my mouth at that moment, so I resorted to downing the ale in one long draft. And that was a mistake, too, as I then found my head swimming along with my vision, and the dinner I had eaten earlier was sitting quite heavily and precariously in my stomach.
'Too pissed to join in,' I laughed, and the moment had passed, thankfully. But I knew I would come back to this thorny little issue.

I didn't wait long. The moment the invitations had arrived we had assumed the shape and tenor of the evening and rather sensibly booked a hotel for the night. It was no accident that it was close enough to the brewery for us to walk back and I tackled Geoff on the walk, once we were away from the rest of them. I say walk, but there was quite a lot of rather undignified weaving, and the trek took us about twice as long as it would have done in sober moments. We didn't even hold on to each other for any kind of support—we had long ago decided never to hold hands in the street, not because of any reluctance to be seen together or indulge ourselves in the dreaded PDA, but for entirely practical reasons—Geoff is well over a foot taller than I and he always said if he held my hand it would look like I was pulling a toilet chain. Our obvious physical differences had always amused us (not to mention the people around us) though we had very much got used to it—he was everything I wasn't: where he was considerably over six feet tall, I struggled to get over five on my tallest days; I was dark, Celtic-heritage dark, with fair skin and freckles in the summer, while he was a proper Nordic blondie; where he was slim to the point of skinny, and gawky and awkward, I was solid, moved easily, sporty; even our dress-styles were at odds—I was always at least tidy and often smart, elegant even, where he had to work hard at putting an outfit together (I had 'consulted' fully over his wardrobe once he started work after college, I can tell you!); I made sure my hair was always well cut and styled, while I had to stop him from just shaving his head when it got too long. Like I said, it suited us. Well, it had up to now.

I wanted very much to phrase the opening question neutrally, even in my drunken haze, so that I got a genuine response from Geoff, rather than a defensive one, and we were nearly halfway back before I found exactly the right words.
'Marianne sounds happy, doesn't she?' I began.
'Yeah, if you like that sort of thing,' he replied, though I detected a bit of sneering in there.
'I don't mean the am-dram stuff,' I continued. 'With Harry, I mean. They seem quite settled.'
'I wonder if he'd say the same,' he laughed.
'Why wouldn't he?'
'Sounds more whipped than settled, if you ask me.'
I had to take care with my tone then, as I found my hackles rising.
'Why whipped?' I ventured.
'Well, she's swanning off doing her own thing, while he's left at home holding the baby, so to speak.'
'He could go out, too,' I suggested rather feebly. 'And how do you

know he doesn't? He might be out every night, for all we know.'
'Didn't sound like it to me,' he said. 'I know I wouldn't like it if you were out every night.'
And my hackles were well and truly up.
'Why not?' I didn't care if he noticed the hostility in my voice.
'Well,' he said evenly, clearly oblivious to my tone, 'what's the point of living together at all if one of us is never there?'
Probably a fair point but I wasn't to be deterred from my quest.
'But it would be all right if you were the one who was always out?'
'Same difference,' was his banal reply.
'So we don't have an equal relationship, then?'
I sensed Geoff becoming cagey before the question was completed —he had never chosen to engage in those conversations about 'us', called them 'new age mumbo-jumbo'—and he took refuge in the unspecified,
'What do you mean?'
'You know what I mean. Are we equal, you and I? Or are you the boss of me?'
'Pah!' he spluttered. 'Chance would be a fine thing.'
And I knew the conversation was over for now. But I was watching from then on.

The very next morning, with both of us trying to reach a degree of consciousness through our monstrous headaches, I watched our morning rituals like an anthropologist. As I graciously signalled him to shower before me, left the bathroom while he cleaned his teeth and repacked his toilet-bag, I was aware of how much I 'gave in' to him, how I treated him like the senior partner. Was it always like this? Was this courtesy or subservience? Was I just noticing for the first time, or was I causing it to happen because I was suddenly aware? On the way down to breakfast he was the one who pressed the button for the lift and led the way to the dining room, it was Geoff who decided silently where we would sit, he who found the menus and handed one to me. He even began to do the ordering as the waitress arrived with a large steaming pot in each hand, ready to pour immediately.

'Coffee, please,' he said brightly, 'for both of us.'
He hadn't checked with me if that was my choice, but then I usually began my day with copious amounts of strong coffee, so I was probably being over-sensitive. Until he went straight on with, 'And two full English, please.'
I was suddenly and disproportionately angry. How dare he order for me? How dare he assume that I wanted whatever he was having? At the same moment, though, I knew to challenge him would be unreasonable: I had allowed him to order for me throughout our relationship; even when I chose my own food he would be the one who spoke it. Yes, I knew I had colluded fully in whatever our relationship was, so, even through the anger, I was careful not to overreact until I had done a great deal more sorting out in my head, not to mention allowing the hangover to subside so I could think rationally.
'Not for me, thank you,' I said, decidedly clipped.
I saw Geoff looking quizzical, and continued without pause,
'Too heavy for me after last night,' and I managed a wan smile, hoping he would assume it was my hangover talking. 'Just some scrambled eggs and a bit of toast, thanks.'
As the waitress left to fetch our order, Geoff smiled (patronisingly? I was reading too much into every gesture now),
'Bit of a bear with a sore head this morning, eh? Man up, woman. You need protein.'
'I'm just being a wussy girl,' I said, keen to return our banter to its previous lightness, for now at least.
'You'll be fine,' he said casually (thoughtlessly? Stop it!) as I reached for my coffee.
'Yeah, I'm sure I will.'
Our breakfast was completed almost in silence, and the long drive home was no more lively. I'm sure Geoff was feeling that we were operating in the companionable silence that was our habit on journeys, but I was using the time to start mentally cataloguing our interaction. I was questioning everything, but the fog of my hangover was, thankfully, enough to keep it inside my head for now. There was too much to think about, too much to analyse,

before I could take any action.

We were soon immersed again in the lives we had begun to carve out for ourselves, but I was determined to test our status quo, and wasted no time. On the first Wednesday after the conferment a small group of people I worked with had decided to go for a drink, 'to avoid the Friday rush lol'. I had been out with them in the past, though not every week, and Jenna always made a point of letting me know when they were going so I could opt in or not. But this week, with my new awareness, I found the invitation more than a little grating.
'Hey, Kel, we're off to The Slug tonight. Fancy it? Or won't old Geoff let you out on a school night?'
Let me out? I was instantly on alert. Had she always phrased it like this? Was she making assumptions about the balance of my relationship with Geoff, or had I led people to believe this was how it was? Is this really how she viewed my relationship, or was she bringing her own baggage into the equation? I knew I was reading far too much into her throwaway comment, and could hardly challenge her – the state of my relationship wasn't even the main subject of the question. I settled for the bland response,
'Lovely, thanks. See you all there, as soon as I've got through this lot,' indicating the untidy heap of paper on my desk.
I immediately sent a text to Geoff, carefully phrased to say as little as possible: *'going for a drink after work'*.
As I pressed send I found myself questioning even those few words. Was my phrasing asking for his permission? Letting him know I was going was at least the polite thing to do – it might alter his evening; it would certainly change our dinner plans, even if that meant just delaying them. For the next hour or so I found myself looking forward to his reply. There would certainly be one, and I wanted to see if he was at all put out. When it came, his reply told me almost nothing:
'don't be too late'.
And I was off again: why shouldn't I be late? Was he trying to limit me? Was he treating me like a little girl who needed reminding to

be responsible? Was he thinking only of himself, not wanting to be on his own for too long? Or was he just being solicitous of my welfare? Maybe he hadn't given a thought to his message at all, and was just acknowledging my own.
I knew I was being unreasonable but really wanted to know what he meant, so I spent a little time working out exactly how to respond.
Finally, I sent back,
'Why shouldn't I be late? What did you have in mind?'
There, that wasn't inflammatory, surely. There's no tone in a text. The pile on my desk had shrunk satisfyingly during the afternoon, and it was almost time to make my way over to the others, most of whom had already gone, when I got his answer,
'Just found a nice bottle of that Beaujolais you like. Thought we could have it with our spag bol.'
Now, was that even a response to my earlier questions, or just his suggestion for our evening? Was it an attempt to entice me away from my planned diversion, or just an alternative? Or was I becoming ridiculous now, looking for offence where none was intended?

The evening was not a pleasant one.

I came home from the pub at the sort of time I would normally after such a casual evening, to find Geoff had waited for me – no dinner cooked, no wine uncorked – and, after the couple of drinks I had had with my friends, I was definitely spoiling for a fight. He greeted me with the sort of comment I had heard from him many times over the years, and which had never appeared sinister or controlling before. But I was ready to read volumes into it, whether they were actually there or not.
'Well, hello there, you dirty stop-out,' he began lightly, no edge to his voice, no tone of accusation or disapproval. But he made the fatal error of checking his watch, and I flew.
'Yes, it's after eight,' I snarled. 'What of it? Is that a problem for you?'

He was clearly unsettled, and immediately became defensive. I mean, I could hardly blame him for that, but I wasn't going to allow him to take the high ground.

'I think the problem's yours,' he said, this time with a definite sharpness, but almost before he had finished speaking I was at him again,

'I don't have a problem. Do you really object to me going out and having a nice time? Or is it just because I didn't take you with me? Is that it?'

He tried to join in, but he was too taken aback to engage with any vigour, while I was thoroughly primed by my afternoon of wondering and my evening of drinking.

'And have you had dinner?'

'Well, no,' he started, 'I was waiting for you...'

'Really? Couldn't manage a bit of spag bol for yourself? Had to wait for the little woman to come home and cook it for you. You sound just like my dad.'

And I could see he was actually stung by the comparison.

'Of course I could manage spag bol. I just thought you might like some, too.' Thought we might eat together.'

He was right, of course, had done nothing wrong, and nothing he hadn't done dozens of times before, but I had spent too much time winding myself up to this challenge to lose momentum now. I didn't allow myself to acknowledge that I didn't know what point I was trying to make any more. Surely I was better than this?

'Right,' I bustled into the kitchen, 'where's the stuff? Let me make the dinner for my lord and master before he wastes away.'

I ignored Geoff's open mouth and slightly hurt expression. He really didn't know where this was coming from, and I'm not sure I did any more. I hadn't even taken off my coat before I set to chopping onions and boiling water. He then made the mistake of following me into the kitchen.

'Come on, Kel, what's the matter? Let's just get a takeaway.'

'And waste all this? Not likely. And then what? 'My girlfriend won't cook my dinner',' said with added whining for effect.

Finally, he put up his hands in surrender and retreated, realising even before I did that there would be no speedy resolution to this nonsense. I think he was just concerned for my sanity at that point.

Dinner was torturously quiet, and I went to bed early with a book, as soon I had ascertained that he was doing the washing up, and made sure my light was out before he came in. I had no idea where this was all going, and was aware that I had already invested far too much energy in this one little notion.

We didn't see each other the next morning, though there was nothing unusual in that – Geoff was usually out of the house before I was even up on a work day - and I was preoccupied all day at work, checking my phone frequently for a message, something from him to give me some clue as to his mood. But there was nothing. I tried not to read anything into that, either – we didn't message each other constantly on a normal day, so why should this one be any different? Well, this would have to wait till I got home, though quite what I was expecting, or hoping for, was not at all clear. After yesterday, nobody was planning on going out after work, so I had no excuse to postpone going home, and I wasn't sure why I had a distinct feeling that I wanted to delay whatever was coming once I got there.

As it turned out, it was the beginning of the end. He opened with, 'Are you better today?' which sent me soaring again, which he tried to ignore, hoping, I assume, that my little storm would eventually blow itself out and I would return to my previous complacency. The trouble was, I now saw that as compliance, while he had every right to expect the previous version of me to resurface. He was a really decent man, and in the back of my mind I knew he was asking if I was alright because he wanted me to be, but I was searching for every offence and his question seemed like disapproval. We were never going to be content and easy with each other again. There was some brief discussion, which reappeared almost daily over the next couple of weeks, but Geoff stayed true to his easy nature, and continued to find it difficult to engage in debate of any emotional depth, despite being thoroughly rattled, while I remained unsettled and challenging. Surprisingly, he was the one who suggested that our relationship had had its day, about three weeks after the initial stupidity.

'Would you rather be on your own? Is that it?' he ventured tentatively after I had stomped about the kitchen making as much noise as possible while throwing things into pans, yet again.

I didn't know whether he meant on my own for now, or on my own permanently, though I suspected the latter, and I needed time to think whether that was really what I wanted after all.

'The kitchen's not big enough for both of us to cook together,' I said lamely, carefully side-stepping what I thought he was hinting at.

I watched him steel himself for broaching the subject more directly than he had ever done in his life.

'No, I mean here, living on your own. Do you want me to go?'

Did I?

'I don't know, do I?'

I could be really childish! I was beginning to dislike myself more and more, but didn't know how to stop the train, and continued,

'What do you want?' I hurled it at him like an accusation. 'Make your own decision.'

'Well, it seems like you don't even like me any more,' speaking more quietly now.

I knew it was really unfair of me to make him feel like that – everybody liked Geoff, it was almost impossible not to.

I thought he was going to cry. Instead, he just withdrew, and I found him in the bedroom a short while later, putting clothes into his large holdall.

'What are you doing?' I asked redundantly and a little aggressively. Even now I couldn't give in, couldn't show my mild panic at what I had precipitated. Why on earth not?

'You don't want me here, clearly, so I'll leave.'

'Where will you go?' I spoke no more softly than before.

'Why do you care?' he said sharply and with some degree of accuracy: if I was driving him away, didn't want to be with him any more, why would I care where he was going?
'Suit yourself,' I said over my shoulder as I left him to it.

He was gone within the half hour, leaving me time to reflect on what had just happened. It hit me like a wet flannel in the face that I had driven him away. I was the one who had started it all, I had moved the goalposts of our relationship, picked and picked at a scab that was probably never there to begin with. And look where it had got me. Surely, I could have explored our roles from within the relationship, should have sorted it out with him, rather than at him. Within ten minutes of him leaving I picked up my phone, wanting to bring him back. But I didn't know if he was too hurt or bewildered to hear that just now, and I was still too far up on my high horse to actually apologise.

The next day I heard a text come in and grabbed my phone, surprised at the little flutter I felt when I saw it was from him. I was then further surprised at the jolt I experienced when I read, *'would it be alright if I come for the rest of my stuff after work on Friday?'* When I found myself disappointed that he hadn't been asking to come home, I nearly cried right there in the office. Instead I sent back a non-committal *'No problem'*. I still didn't know if that control nonsense had been in my head, whether the unequal relationship theory was a figment of my imagination. Well, if that were the case I didn't deserve a relationship, was far too immature for one, so maybe it was all for the best.

On Friday I went out for a drink with the gang, not wanting to be there when he came. I didn't want to ask myself why. Was it because I thought I might weaken and ask him to stay? Or because I didn't want to see his pain, or worse, find that he had none. So I was glad to find my timing was perfect – he had been and cleared out every last reminder of himself from our flat before I got home. I saw immediately how thoughtful and fair he had been – he had taken nothing that wasn't his, and had even left me all the 'our' stuff – kitchen things, dvd's we had bought together and so on - while leaving nothing that he should have taken so I didn't have to clear up after him. He was decent to the end. Then, just as I was nodding to myself that it was all for the best, I saw, on the little hall table we used for post and the occasional vase of flowers, his front-door key. For a moment I just stared at it, until its significance seemed to launch itself at me, and I found myself howling. And without him there to calm me I just kept right on howling until I cried myself to sleep. What had I done?

2.

So, time to learn to live alone, and that would be an entirely new experience for me. As a child, of course, I lived at home with my (very traditional) parents and siblings (one of each), then I had always shared rooms at college, and then straight to this flat with Geoff. Perhaps this was my chance to grow up a bit, get to know myself, work out what I actually wanted from life, to think about it for a change, instead of just sort of letting life happen to me. And maybe turn myself into a nicer person! I knew I was a decent soul underneath, but I didn't like myself very much right now, and that had to change.

The first obstacle, however, was Beth. Dear, sensible, grown-up Beth, my best friend since high school. She was the one all the girls aspired to be like and all the boys fancied (though from a distance!). But she would have none of that coupling nonsense, having chosen at a remarkably young age to devote her copious energies to getting good qualifications and a sparkling career, to setting up the life she had decided she wanted. Her work ethic and determination set the tone for all of us at school, and I credit her influence on my own; she kept me working, partly in healthy competition – who could get through the most work, or achieve higher marks – and partly just by example: anybody who wanted to spend time with her, and I did, must be prepared to spend at least some of it learning, putting the work first. Oh, she knew how to enjoy herself, and was always the best company, but frivolity took its place in the queue behind work and future. For her, relationships were either a distraction from her goals or a little diversion between them. She had never had a boyfriend (or a girlfriend for that matter) who lasted more than a few weeks, always her choice, and lived alone happily with a small shaggy-faced rescue mutt called Elvis, in a beautiful third-floor flat with a balcony and views across the park on the edge of town. She also had the woolliest job-title in the world – Project Manager. While still in her teens she had made the decision never to work for anybody else, so she was self-employed, going off wherever the work was, often for weeks at a time, yes, managing projects. She spent a lot of time on trains or in her car, but she never complained as it was 'good thinking time', not to mention all charged to the client. I had long ago given up asking her for details about whichever project she was on, as they were so varied: if a company wanted to change something she would tender for the role of effecting that change, and her quickly-established reputation for competence and professionalism meant that she was never out of work. In fact, more than one company had paused their projects to coincide with when she would be available to manage them – she was that sought-after. Often the project would be the introduction of a new IT system within a company, and she would be the one who oversaw such things as audits, procurement and resourcing, then training and implementation, all of which had made her a whizz with technology, of course; sometimes it would be a big move she was organising – packing and transport, and she quickly became adept at getting the best deals for her clients; she had even done more than one building project – meeting with architects and planners, ensuring buildings were fit for purpose, then dealing with contractors and materials, and she could talk technically with them all now. She was no jill of all trades, either – she made sure she mastered everything. She was very good at her job, and loved it all.

Her unwavering confidence in her own lifestyle choices, however, didn't mean that she ever disapproved of other people's, and she was always available as a sounding-board or critical friend, especially to me. When I was leaving college she was the one I went to for career discussions, it was her advice I sought when trying to decide on my professional direction, and she had never failed me yet. But she was unerringly honest without ever being offensive – a neat trick for those who can manage it. While most people found that refreshing, I knew she wouldn't sugar-coat any judgement she might have of me, and she had always liked Geoff, thought he was good for me, his very steadiness a calming influence, so I found myself dreading the inevitable phone call to let her know what had happened, what I had done. I wasn't disappointed. Once I had outlined the main points, her opening salvo was,

'You twat.'

'Thanks for that,' I droned miserably.

'Don't you sit there feeling sorry for yourself. You did it. You sabotaged your own relationship, it seems to me.'

'That's not fair,' I tried to convince myself more than her. 'We're all only fifty percent of any relationship, remember. He contributed.'

'How? By being himself, behaving how he always has?' she reasoned impeccably. 'He didn't change, didn't do anything different. You did. It was you.'

'You always take his side.' I was actually pouting now, even though she couldn't see me.

'My bro,' she said. 'Of course.'

I wasn't the only one who noticed how alike they were, physically at least. Both tall, slim, naturally blond (though enhanced, shall we say, in Beth's case), and they had been asked if they were brother and sister more than once when we were all together.

'Who else will defend him against the mighty you when you're in this mood?'

'I was hoping for a bit of support,' I whined childishly.

'And you'll get it from me, all you need, you know that. But do you think support looks like unmitigated approval? Am I supposed to tell you you did the right thing? That everything will be alright? It was all for the best? Tell you what, how about I just sit and cluck and pat you on the head while you pour out your soul?'

'Well, everybody else has been really sympathetic,' I whined again, thinking of the people I worked with, none of whom I would call real friends, and none of whom had any detailed picture of my relationship in the first place, so they were not in a position to offer more than superficial sympathy.

'Well, stick with them, then,' she offered with a laugh in her voice. 'I'm sure they'll help you recover.'

'You're mean,' I resorted to the childish rather than concede she was, as always, completely correct.

'Come on over tonight,' she laughed again. 'I'll cook you something comforting and you can sit like a bag of dripping on my sofa for a couple of hours. We can even get drunk if you like.'

'I'd like that.'

'But you're getting this one evening. That's it. I'll help you as much as you like, but I won't sit and listen to weeks of whining when your injury has been so clearly self-inflicted. OK?'

'OK,' I said. She was a proper mate.

The next hurdle was Christmas. My family always took the family thing seriously and not spending the whole holiday period there from Christmas Eve until after Boxing Day was not an option. Not that I minded: my parents were generous and decent, if a little dull and traditional, my sister and brother and I still quite close, and mostly I enjoyed their company. I wouldn't actually want to live with any of them now, but it was usually a happy place to relax and be waited on for a few days when everything else was shut down. For the last couple of years, though, I had had Geoff's family to consider along with my own, and we had sort of shared ourselves out between the two homes. Sadly, they lived too far apart to allow us to see them on alternate days, for example, so it was one family one year and the other the next. It was my parents' turn this year, and I didn't know if I was pleased about that or not. On the one hand, if I had been scheduled to be at Geoff's, I could have put off telling them about our recent history and just stayed at home on my own, or maybe found a group of other singles doing the same and joined in. But I knew instinctively that would probably not be healthy to have so much time to brood, and would leave me feeling more than sorry for myself, so I decided to 'fess up and meet my family obligations. I spared myself a lecture, though, by not telling them the details or circumstances, and made it clear I didn't want to talk about it. They had no idea I had brought it all on myself and were only too keen to spare my feelings.

By the end of Boxing Day I was ready to get away from the guilt of allowing them to assume it was Geoff who had left me. They were upset both on my behalf and their own – like everybody else I knew, they all liked him – and made it clear they couldn't understand how anybody could be foolish or heartless enough to abandon their precious girl. This meant special personalised pampering for the whole time I was there, despite rather knowing sideways glances from my sister who didn't buy my Greta Garbo act, piling on the guilt more with every mug of hot chocolate and extra slice of cake. I was glad I'd gone, but still happy to get back home and back to work – I was close to being stifled. Luckily the New Year found us busier than ever, and I was only too ready to put in long hours and fill my head with anything that wasn't Geoff.

Meanwhile, Beth was filling my weekends and evenings with a busy mix of cultural pursuits and mindless activity: we went to the cinema, cooked for each other at home, visited museums and galleries, and even on one occasion managed a jolly hour in the park with a picnic on the frozen grass. I was pleased she wasn't working away at the moment – it was good to have her with me, mopping up after the mess I had made, as usual.

By springtime I was starting to face the world with, if not joy, at least a reluctant resignation. While I didn't actually relish it, couldn't call myself actually happy, I was starting to get used to my new life and the satisfaction of making all my own decisions. It all still felt a little empty, though, with no-one to share it all with. I found myself consciously looking for something more substantial to fill my time, a project. Yes, I needed a project.

I discussed it with Beth, of course. She suggested volunteering, so I looked first into serving in the local charity shop. That idea was dismissed quite quickly, though, as my Monday to Friday job meant I could do only weekends and all of those sessions were filled with students looking to beef up their cv's. The same problem ruled out feeding hospital patients, acting as a Responsible Adult, and reading with schoolchildren – I would never be available at the times they needed me.

Finally, Beth came up with politics. I had actually gone to a public meeting a year or so before, when someone had proposed a local by-pass. They had first flagged up the idea of a flyover, and I had ghastly visions of our whole town, our rural oasis, being consumed by a monstrous shadow as the road towered over us all and cut us off from the rest of the world. I turned up at the Town Hall with dozens of other concerned residents, and found myself actually addressing the meeting at one point. We were all relieved when the Council recognised the deep objections to their idea, and abandoned it, and I had a moment of self-congratulation at the small part I had played in allowing our voices to be heard. Beth reminded me of this and it struck a little chord. OK, maybe this was what I needed, to get involved in other people's issues, think about someone other than myself.

I started with research, first getting onto the Council's website to find out all their meetings were open to the public, so I would begin by attending a few to see how things went. I knew I would need to acquire knowledge and understanding of the issues, and fast, and assumed my good memory would serve me well when it needed to, but, as a starting point, I called into the newsagent at the end of my road to arrange for the local newspaper to be delivered every week – I knew they often reported on Council business as well as detailing local events and issues. Next, I looked at how I could be elected to office if I ever thought the time was right. That was slightly more complex as I needed sponsors to propose me, then offices and meeting rooms and all manner of periphery that I knew nothing about yet, and the received wisdom was telling me I needed to join a recognised party to handle all that for me. Having been brought up in a politically-neutral (naïve?) family I had always been a floating voter, inclined to vote on single issues or personalities rather than tribally, so that was going to be difficult: how could I choose between the parties, when I found fault and credit in all of them? In the end, I decided to just get to some meetings and hope my path would emerge.

The first meeting I went to should have been a dull affair. I plumped for the first I found listed, and it was to be the Planning Committee, dealing mostly with permission for people's porches and extensions and some 'change of use' applications. The Town Hall Conference Room I was directed to was about the size of a decent living-room, comfortable if utilitarian, a large table at its centre, with well-upholstered chairs around it and more of the same chairs in a short row against one wall. This was the public 'gallery', and I took a seat along with two other people, both of whom, it transpired, were there to hear consideration of their own applications. I was expecting a room full of grey hair and tweed, and was pleasantly surprised to find the closest thing to diversity that our town had to offer, a range of ages and 'types' within the handful of attendees. There was a shiny if distracted young woman in a sharp suit, one large middle-aged African-Caribbean man in jeans, one more elderly Asian man (yes, in a slightly frayed tweed jacket) – and a middle-aged woman in a loud floral dress with a cardigan. I looked all of them up later, to discover that the young woman was the deputy head of our local high school (shouldn't she have been on the Education Committee?), the two men were both businessmen – the one in jeans ran the town's only Caribbean restaurant, the older one had a flooring warehouse in the retail park – and the elderly woman was a prematurely-retired office clerk who had made the choice to 'put something back into the community' now she had the time. At the end of the table, however, was the brightest pair of eyes and the most immediately energetic human being I think I have ever encountered: Tim Byrne, young, dynamic, mesmerising and brisk, the Chair of this Committee.

I'm ashamed to report that I took in almost nothing of what was discussed that evening. Not only was the business largely as dull as I had predicted, but I was so struck by this ball of energy in the Chair I could barely focus on anything else. I did notice, however, his laudable attention to the particulars of each item in front of him – he seemed to have memorised every detail, and gave the impression that he really cared for each individual. More than once he reminded the Committee that there were real people behind each of these papers; at one point he was challenged by Old Man Tweed with 'is this the sort of thing Ordnage really wants?', only to silence him with, 'if the home-owner wants it then who are we to say they shouldn't have it? We won't be living there.' Every application bar one (which just needed clarification about some proposed materials to be probably ratified at the next meeting) was granted, and in little more than half the time we had been told the meeting would last. So he was as efficient as he was charismatic.

At the end of the business part of the evening he unleashed a killer smile that took in the whole room and asked 'if nobody has anything else?', then stood and put on the jacket that had been hanging on the back of his chair. 'So,' he continued with barely a pause, 'anyone for the George? Kick-off's in ten.' There was a murmur from the table, a mix of 'right-oh's and 'not tonight's as I realised he was including the public gallery in his invitation. Did I want to go and watch the match with a pint in the local with a group of people I didn't know at all? Well, why not? I'd only be doing the same thing at home on my own. The other two sitting with me both declined without words, and sloped off as I moved towards the central table.
'Love to,' I said advancing. 'Kelly Arben,' offering a hand.
Tim took it briefly and said, 'Great. You can walk over with us.'

That was a given, actually, as I'd come on the bus to the Town Hall, knowing how notorious the parking was around it.
'Ashraf?' he continued, addressing Old Man Tweed. 'You coming?'
'Not tonight, thanks, Tim - not eaten yet.'
'You can grab a bar meal down there,' cajoled Tim.
'Nah, Beena will have my guts if I don't go home. She'll have been cooking all afternoon. You know what she's like.'
There was a knowing smile between them – this was obviously well-trodden ground.
Brief introductions were made on the short walk to the George, so at least I knew who I'd be drinking with: Tim, of course, plus John Placide, the restaurant owner, and Audrey DeVane, she of the floral frock. Presumably the deputy head had a load of marking to do or something. I was mildly impressed when we made our way into the pub, which was already pretty full so close to kick-off time, only to find an unoccupied table in prime position to the right of the giant screen. On it was a small plastic menu-holder with a large white card stuck in it, and on the card it said 'RESERVED for Mr Tim Byrne'. Now that was planning! Around the table were two stools and two chairs – he had even booked the right number of seats (though probably more by good guesswork or experience than preparation). As I made to sit on one of the stools I felt a hand in the middle of my back as Tim redirected me towards one of the chairs, saying,
'No, that'll get uncomfortable. Take this one.'
'Why should you be uncomfortable instead of me?' I twittered.
'Oh, don't worry about me. I'll be up and down.'
So we sat in chivalrous arrangement, the men on stools and the women on the comfy chairs. Funny, particularly after the path I had taken with Geoff, I wasn't offended or even alerted by it.
'I'll get the first round,' said Tim, bounding towards the bar. 'What'll it be, Kelly?'
I didn't have to think – I had seen the label in the window on my way in.
'A pint of the Old Original, please.'
I knew that was the nearest I'd get to a decent ale around here.

'Good choice!' he said, then, 'Usual, John? Audrey?'
They both nodded, then turned their attention to me.
'So, what brings you here?' asked John pleasantly. 'Did you have an application in?'
'No,' I said rather tentatively, beginning to wonder if I hadn't been a little foolish to join in this jaunt – was I to be grilled? 'I just wanted to see how it all worked, you know, Council stuff.'
'Like what you see?' Audrey joined in. 'We're not very exciting, are we?'
'Efficient, though. The website said the meeting would last about two hours.'
'Ah,' said John, with clear approval, 'that's Tim for you. He likes his business brisk.'
By which time the man himself was back with the drinks, and we raised them to each other and to kick-off. Perfect timing.
We had a second during the first half, and Audrey left at half time, with a pleasant 'nice to meet you, dear' as she handed me her Council business card. The match was more entertaining than eventful, but the partisan crowd around us made conversation more than difficult, and John followed her, also handing me his card, once a third goal had rendered the final result inevitable. So I was left with just Tim. Even if I had wanted to leave it would have felt rude to leave him alone, so I got us our last couple of drinks and we finished them off as the final whistle blew. Thankfully the noise around us subsided then into merely conversation, and Tim turned his chair to face me.
'So, tell me about Miss Kelly Arben. I assume it's Miss.'
I was immediately uncomfortable. That's a hard question. Usually, I would rely on context in designing an answer. I would know how to frame it at a job interview, for example, but I didn't know what he was expecting in this setting. Was it just a conversation-opener, or genuine interest? I decided quickly to treat it professionally, as the least intrusive option, and began with the broadest of biographical notes.
'I'm twenty-three, an account manager at Bellows, and I grew up around here.'

What else did he want?

'So what brought you to us this evening?' he went on, twinkling animatedly. He made it sound as if he really wanted to know about me.

'Curiosity, really,' I ventured without inspiration. 'I just wanted to see how these things worked, you know, the Council, Committees and the like.'

'Ah, I see,' he said, as if I'd just revealed a great secret. 'And did we measure up?'

Measure up to what? I had no preconceptions, so nothing to measure the proceedings against. Again, I went with the answer that would give the least away, though I was not sure what I was holding onto.

'It was fine,' I said blandly, 'interesting.'

At that he laughed heartily.

'You can call us many things on the old Planning Committee, but I would never have put interesting first.'

I was embarrassed at the thought that I had insulted him, but he didn't appear to be offended, far from it – he was still chuckling as if I had told a good joke.

'Well,' he went on, sensing my discomfort, I think, 'there's nothing much contentious about a few loft conversions, is there?'

'No,' I protested just a little, 'I learned a lot.'

'Will you come again?'

'Well, I don't know if I'll come to another Planning Committee, but I'd like to learn about how it all works, the Council I mean.'

'You should come to a full Council Meeting some time, see some real horse-trading! They can be quite fiery.' He said this as if contention was something to be proud of or sought after.

'Maybe I will. When is the next one?'

'Next Thursday at 7. They're usually on Thursdays, though I'm not sure why.' 'And when's the next one after that?'

My diary was hardly packed right now, but I still wanted to make sure I hadn't got anything else planned before I committed myself.

'I haven't checked the schedule beyond next week, but they're more or less monthly, with a bit of a break in the summer. Will you come?'

'I may well,' I said, reading a warm welcome in his smile, and thinking ahead rather too imaginatively. 'And now, if you'll excuse me, I think it was time I was off.'

'Must you go?' he said, pouting a little, and I'm sure I wasn't imagining a dash of invitation in there.

'It's a bit late for a school night,' I smiled back.

'OK, then,' he said, standing chivalrously, 'how are you getting home?'

'Same way I came, I guess – the number 42.'

'Oh, no,' he said, grabbing his coat. 'I can't have young women walking these dark streets alone.'

I don't know why I didn't bristle at the 'wrong place wrong time' implication.

'Come on, my car's in the Town Hall car park.

'Oh, no, I wouldn't want to take you out of your way.'

'You don't know where my way is!' he laughed again. He laughed a lot.

I didn't take much persuading. I had never liked walking on my own after dark, and our buses were not known for their reliability. What could go wrong?

I think conversations are often more honest when we don't have to look each other in the eye, so it was in the car on our short journey to my flat that my real reason for turning up tonight emerged. Not that I was actually hiding it, I just needed to try it on for size for a while before making a fool of myself with my lofty pretensions. I mean, imagine me seeking office - the very definition of imposter syndrome!

'So, come on,' he said as he drove out of the car park, 'why are you so interested in us? Ooh, maybe you're really a journalist wanting to expose us!'

He was making me laugh again, putting me at my ease. So this time I answered his question with a straight answer.

'Well,' I started, looking out of the window away from him, 'I was thinking of maybe getting involved,' which made me feel a little

foolish all over again. But he reassured me immediately.
'Good for you! So what are you fancying?' (Don't ask, Tim!) 'A bit of Party work, or volunteering? We always need good people.'
Was he ever anything but enthusiastic?
'I don't know about that,' I laughed with him. 'I've no idea what I might be good at. I just thought I ought to get involved in my community. And as to which party, I've really no clue. Aren't they all as bad as each other?'
'Probably,' he sparkled again, but this time I noticed a definite shift in tone, as if he was thinking of something. Oh, I don't mean his mind was elsewhere, just as if other ideas were growing there alongside our conversation.
I carried on, 'I suppose I ought to join a party, but how does any of us know which is the best fit for us? I need to find out what they've all done for us round here. I could only be a part of one with a conscience.'
'Good for you,' he said again, but there wasn't much of a smile to accompany this one, and he didn't continue.
We were almost outside my front door by this time and I pointed ahead,
'Just under that lamppost would be perfect, thanks.'
As I moved to step out of the car I felt a hand on my arm. It didn't feel at all tense or threatening so I turned back towards him questioningly.
'Look, Kelly, I have an idea,' he started thoughtfully. 'But this isn't the time and place. Can I come and talk to you?'
Now he had really piqued my interest, but I preferred cagey for now, having no idea what he might be suggesting.
'What about?'
'Parties. Political Parties. The right one for you, maybe.'
'OK, sounds intriguing. When?'
'I'm actually free tomorrow evening, if that's good for you.'
I didn't have to check my diary this time: Beth was working away again, so I knew I was free, and said so.
'Where shall we meet?'
'I know it sounds a bit shady, but I'd rather not have this

conversation out in public, not till it's all firmed up.'

'Till what's all firmed up?' I had no idea what he was talking about, but I couldn't possibly let this drop till I knew what he meant. I was already drawn into this intrigue. 'Is it something illegal?'

He laughed at that, which was reassuring.

'Not even unethical, I promise.' And I believed him.

'OK,' I took the proverbial bull by the horns, 'do you want to come to me?'

'That would be great,' he agreed. 'What time do you get home from work?'

'I'm usually back before 6. I can make sure I am if that's a good time for you.'

'Great,' he said, 'shall I bring fish and chips?'

That was a surprise – I hadn't even thought about dinner, but I found myself agreeing anyway. He handed me his card,

'In case you get a better offer,' he sparkled.

As I climbed out of the car and made my way into the flat I couldn't help wondering what I was getting myself into, but was equally aware that I was actually childishly excited. Let's see what tomorrow evening would bring.

3.

That night I Googled him, of course, only to find out very little. There was not much more out there, in fact, than what I already knew. I didn't know if it was telling or not that I couldn't find many personal details beyond his age and education, but the mystery made him even more intriguing.

Tim arrived right on time, exactly at 6 o'clock, steaming bag of food in one hand and a rather smart giant messenger bag in the other. He was more casually dressed than the evening before, when he had been in a well-cut 3-piece suit. Tonight it was chinos and a pale blue polo shirt with a soft black leather jacket. I was still in my work gear, so looked like a stereotype of a secretary – navy suit, crisp white shirt and low heels. I kicked them off as we made our way to my little kitchen table and decanted our improvised dinner onto plates. I got us each a glass of water, but I wasn't in the mood for patience, and curiosity took over even before the first mouthful.

'So, what was this great idea?' I said as the first chip went in.
'Ooh, you don't waste any time, do you?' he grinned as he sprinkled the salt.

I didn't want to admit that I'd thought about little else since he mentioned it last night. I had had another of those daft days at work, where I went through the motions, functioning almost by remote, because I was too preoccupied with what this evening might bring. I was glad there had been no major queries or difficulties requiring clear thinking and incisive decision-making – I would have failed!

'Well, you intrigued me,' I said, and waited for him to broach whatever it was he had in mind for me. It was a long, long speech, and I listened intently, growing more excited with every sentence, as the heat leached out of our food.

'Let me start by taking you back a few years. I have always been drawn to politics, and while I was at university – I studied law, by the way – I joined all the affiliated groups. Yes, I know, before you say anything, that was probably the most unethical thing I did. But I wasn't spying for any one over the others – I truly wanted to find out what they each stood for, what they represented, and I thought that doing it from the inside was the quickest way to do that. But none of them was an exact fit for me, and they were all clichés. I have a leaning to the left, always have had, from my parents, I suppose, but the university Labour group was all hairy protest and pc rhetoric and a lot of beer.' That sounded pretty perfect to me! 'The Conservative crowd was no better – a bunch of over-privileged hoorays using abusive terminology to dismiss what they saw as the rabble, but without actually doing anything. I couldn't take any of the one-platform parties seriously - you know, the Greens, the Christian Democrats, the Independent this-that-and-everything-else - so by the end of my first year at uni I had gravitated to the Lib-Dems. They seemed to voice the middle ground in most issues, were innately moderate, and didn't make me angry or bored like some of the others. But even then I knew they didn't say everything I wanted to say, and my membership lapsed before the year was out.'

He was supremely articulate and engaging, and this introduction was so polished I knew it was not the first time he had delivered it.

'Now, I should tell you here about my mate Russell. Comes from Rutland and went back home there after uni. Russell was another law student, like me, and with similar views about politics in general and university politics in particular. He had also flirted with all the groups and found none really filled in the blanks for him. He was the one who first came up with the idea of starting our own party.'

I was riveted now.

'Just like that?' I said through a mouthful of fish. 'A whole new party?'

'It was surprisingly easy,' he wasn't eating now. 'As quickly as that.'

He clicked his fingers.

'We just sorted a half-arsed manifesto, got a few mates to join in, put out a lot of flyers, and stood for election on all the student councils. We made sure we were very visible and active, socially as well as politically, and the numbers swelled quickly. In our last year we were the number one group at the university – more members, more officers, more visual and active than all the others put together.'

'Wow,' I said quietly.

'And it worked. We campaigned for, and got, new professional librarians, better cleaning in the halls and grounds, lecturer appraisal by students, more transparent selection processes, and coursework elements included in finals. We were a force to be reckoned with.'

'In a year?' I was in awe.

'Yep,' he said with obvious pride, 'well, just over the year. And the party is still there, still growing, still active and strong. We left the university far more healthy than when we had arrived. And now we knew we could do it.'

'And does this new party of yours have a name?'

'We are the Guardians.'

I laughed, 'That's a bit grand, isn't it?'

'It fits our philosophy. We needed to avoid anything that marked us as particularly left or right, and wanted people to feel they mattered, were important, that they were being heard, each one of them as an individual. And that we would be the ones to make sure they were looked after. We even thought out a strap-line, well, a sort of mission statement to go with it, one that says it all in a few words.'

I waited for him to tell me what it was, but he just smiled at me like a matador about to deliver the coup de grace. This was going to be a knockout.

I tipped my head to one side quizzically and said, 'Well? Are you going to tell me what it is?'

'It's the simplest thing,' he said, clearly trying not to be too smug, 'it's, 'We'll look after you'.'

I had been expecting something seismic, astounding, and this simple little statement was far from that. A brief thought fluttered through my brain that I should probably have found it too trivial for serious politics, maybe even laughable, but he was completely sincere, even getting a little bit intense now, so I couldn't laugh out loud without looking like a simpleton, or a doubter. And I really didn't want him to think I would doubt him – he was so convincing. I knew I was hooked, and so did he. He finally took a breath then, and started on the food in front of him. But I could tell there was more to come, so I plunged on,

'So, what next?'

I think he was happy to be asked to keep going, and put down the next chip. Oh, dear – was my interest going to cause him to starve? But he was really on a roll now, and leaned towards me with his elbows on the table, looking for all the world like a real politician.

'Well, Russell and I see ourselves as the vanguard of real political change in this country. He's done in his home town what I've done here – got himself elected onto the Council, and is very busy heading Committees and making his voice heard locally. And there are another half a dozen of us around the country doing the same thing.'

'And you're all Guardians, is that it? Why haven't I ever heard of you?

'Because we're not really Guardians, not yet.'

I was confused, and said so. 'So which party do you belong to, all

of you? Surely you have to represent somebody.'
'I'm slightly ashamed to say I took the Independent route first, as did Russell and all the others. That was part of our plan. If we are ever as successful as we hope to be, no, expect to be, we didn't want the baggage of accusations of turncoat on our cv's. Anybody who 'crosses the floor' is always viewed with suspicion. It would follow us around, not to mention taint the message.'

'But how do you get yourself elected without the backing of one of the big guys?'
'It's easier than you'd think. There are actually far fewer people than you might imagine who want to do this job: it's not easy, the hours are long, and all on top of working a proper job. And nobody thinks they're qualified enough, even if they feel the need to serve their community. We just put our names forward and pay the deposit. You can always find somebody who's prepared to propose you.'

I was thoughtful now, most of my fish and chips still on my plate.
'So what's next?' I asked, genuinely wanting to know.
'Next year's Council elections. This is why your timing is so perfect – you've come to us at exactly the right time. We're going to need good bodies on the ground.'
'Go on,' I said a little tentatively. Suddenly I wasn't unlike all those people he'd mentioned, the ones who believed themselves to be under-qualified for office. I hoped he wasn't asking me to stand for election. Now I'd seen him operate I knew my previous pretensions were just that.
'Well, we're going to declare ourselves openly this time – the Guardians, out and proud. Finally, no pretending, no waiting in the shadows. We're hoping the fact that we've been serving already, and hopefully doing a good job, will stand us in good stead. We've made sure we're highly visible and vocal, meeting as many constituents personally as we can, getting our names and faces out there. We've established enough of a track record for people to vote for us on our merits, as individuals regardless of

party affiliation, fingers crossed. And we want to take as many people with us as we can. Then, next stop, national recognition.'

His eyes were glowing. I could tell he believed every word he was saying, and his plan felt entirely plausible. I had never witnessed such drive, such confidence and ambition before, and I didn't know what to say. I do know I'd have voted for him on the spot! Instead I looked down and paid a little attention to my plate while I thought about it. It really was a lot to take in. But, no matter how charismatic and persuasive he was (and he was!) I knew I couldn't just plunge in and start working with or campaigning for somebody I had just met. I didn't even know what he stood for, not beyond a simplistic strap-line, anyway. I looked up to find him watching me, but, far from being uncomfortable, it felt as if he was waiting for my response. Actually more than that, it felt as if he was seeking my approval.
Finally, 'Can I read this manifesto?'

He reached down into the bag on the floor beside his chair and pulled out half a dozen pages stapled together unassumingly. It was so readily to hand it felt as if he'd been waiting for me to ask. He handed it to me without a word, and I saw a tiny glimpse of vulnerability. So this was his Achilles' heel - his manifesto; was it going to live up to all the promise? Was the promise no more than hype? I studied the front cover for a moment as if it held all the answers, then set it to one side of my plate.
'I assume I can keep this, read it at my leisure?'
'Of course. But please remember it's only a draft. All comments welcome. We want it to be ready before campaigning starts for real, so we've got a few weeks. Then,' and he was really sparkling now, 'welcome aboard.'
I laughed, 'Blimey, you're sure of yourself!'
'Yes, I am, but mostly it's this I'm sure of,' and he tapped, well, almost stroked the document on the table.
'This has the power to change things that have needed changing for a long time.'

I knew I would be reading it as soon as he had left. I didn't know if this manifesto could move mountains, but I was sure Tim and his friends could.

He didn't stay long after that, just long enough to finish off his dinner and put the wrappers in the bin, and I wasn't sorry – I wanted to start reading as soon as possible. At the door he kissed my cheek on the way out.

'I'm really glad you came to the meeting yesterday, Kelly,' and the way he said it made me feel almost like he'd been waiting for me, just me, to join his crusade.
'Me, too,' I agreed, and I was telling the truth.
I think I might have found my project.

4.

The next weeks were a bit of a blur, as I threw myself into the local election campaign with more vigour than I had probably applied to anything in my life before. I began by getting through the manifesto, as I assumed it would tell me more about what they really stood for, what they were committed to, than just talk, which was always at the mercy of the manipulative or half-decent actor. I had finished it within minutes of Tim leaving my flat, and I liked what I read. (In fact, I enjoyed reading it so much that I determined to seek out those of other parties for comparison.) It began with a short bullet-pointed list of generalities outlining the overarching goals and guiding principles of the new political party, and it looked less pretentious in print than hearing it in your own kitchen for the first time. It was a slightly more detailed version of the 'we'll look after you' strapline with which Tim had originally charmed me, and I found myself nodding approval as I read each point; it was filled with 'rights of the individual', 'every person', 'each of us' and 'personal responsibility' – a list of the ways in which they intended to look after each one of us, and not just as groups. Next came their longer-term aims, which they had entitled 'All Our Futures'. This was a similarly brief expression of their utopian vision for everybody, and now I found myself chuckling as I realised how happily I responded to pretentious and grandiose language in the face of such noble sentiments. It was laid out in clearly-labelled sections, such as 'education' (let the professionals make the decisions), 'health' (preserve and extend the NHS, with a particular focus on community medicine), and 'constitution' (House of Lords reform and lowering the voting age). The final section, called 'Ordnage's Tomorrow', was a sort of addendum, a couple of pages setting out the local issues

Tim wanted the Council to address: the by-pass raised its head again, but excluded the flyover option; improvement to transport networks was in there; a complex integration of local schools into one 'superschool' was interesting, if slightly worrying, though I couldn't say why it bothered me. I assumed his colleagues across the country each had a different set to reflect their own local priorities.

Apart from jotting a few notes in the margins, and correcting a couple of typos, I did very little else that evening. I did ring Beth, of course, to tell her about our 'meeting', but instead of sharing gossip I found myself reading almost the entire manifesto to her over the phone. I loved the simplicity of its ideas, and its thoughtful readability. Beth found it less appealing, however, and rang off with a promise to speak again shortly, 'when your evangelical zeal has levelled out into good old-fashioned hero-worship'. I knew she was mocking me, but her derision was always affectionate so I laughed with her. Before I went to bed I typed the few pages onto a data-stick, including my corrections and suggestions; not only have I always found such mindless copying relaxing, but it enabled me to commit detail to memory – this visual trick was one of the main reasons I was so good at dates and statistics. I suppose it is the modern version of the old Chinese proverb about doing and remembering.

The next day I took the data-stick containing the Guardians manifesto into work and, in my lunch-break (I was too professional to use company time for personal crusades) I used the sophisticated software our design team had installed at Bellows to mock up what I hoped was an attractive cover for it. Of course, it wasn't meant to be anything definitive – I had no idea if the party had an official symbol, or preferred colours – but I hoped it would make the whole thing look more professional. I created two different layouts, set them up with a range of background colours, then ran them through the publishing software to complete what I hoped was a more professional-looking brochure.

I checked with Dorrett, my boss, that she didn't mind me taking a few sheets of paper, and printed them off, ready to take to the Council meeting on Thursday. I was a bit more smug than I should have been – it wasn't much more than a bit of typing – but found myself looking forward to showing Tim what I had done. I guess I wanted him to see that I had taken him and his ideas seriously.

Thursday finally came, and I rushed home from work as if I had a date. I grabbed a sandwich and a shower and then stood in front of my wardrobe trying to select the right outfit for this evening. It was at this moment, by chance, that Beth rang me.
'So,' she began, 'looking forward to this evening, then?'
'More than I should, I'm sure,' I replied. 'I'm trying to decide what to wear right now.'
'You're what?' she said, and I could hear the gentle mocking in her tone. 'Who cares what you wear?'
'I know, alright. Stop it.' I knew what she was thinking.
'You're hilarious. Just throw on some jeans. Nobody's looking at you.'
'So why am I nervous?' I asked, probably rhetorically.
'Do you really want me to answer that?'
I didn't.
'I wish I wasn't in bloody Newcastle this week. I'd love to come and meet this paragon.'
'I'm sure you will,' I said, confident already that I was in this, whatever it turned out to be, for the long haul.
She ended the conversation with,
'Look, I can't stop. I was just checking in on you. Now I know you're still quite barking I'll let you get on. Don't forget the full slap, eh?'
'Sod off, doubter. I'll speak to you at the weekend,' as I turned back to the monumental task of finding what I wanted to wear.

After all that, the Council meeting was quite dull, until the very last, that is; Tim was wrong – no fireworks or mud-slinging – just a large group of quite professional grown-ups checking each other's work and making sure the town was safe and well run. It was held in the main council chamber, a beautiful and Gothically-ornate room on the first floor of the Town Hall, reached by climbing a magnificent marble staircase. The richly-carpeted chamber was dominated by a huge polished table covered in papers and surrounded by grand chairs, all occupied. The public gallery was actually that – a gallery overlooking the chamber, and accessed from the floor above. There were uglier places I could think of to be bored. There were only three of us up here, one of whom I recognised as a young reporter from the local paper, notebook and pencil in hand. The meeting began, spot on the advertised time of 7 o'clock, with very standard stuff that any meeting would recognise: adopting minutes of the previous meeting, absentees and their excuses and so on. Next came a long address from the Mayor, Cllr Chandni Patel, which contained a surprising amount of personal stuff: she congratulated one Councillor on the birth of his new baby, thanked several others for attending a couple of her charity events, and led a lot of rather smug self-congratulation all round at the news that the Standards Committee had notched up a full three years since anybody here had been cautioned or sanctioned for inappropriate behaviour. (The little cynical voice inside me couldn't help wondering if it was, rather, that they just hadn't been caught.) It was during this that I first caught Tim's eye. I was ridiculously pleased - I'm sure I actually blushed - when he glanced up and found me looking down at him, and his slight nod and warm smile told me he was pleased I was there. After that, each Committee had to report back on their meetings and decisions since the last full Council, with questions at the end 'from the floor', and there were a few procedural issues I didn't understand or care about.

The last item was where it all changed. It was listed in the agenda as 'Motions', but there were no details, other than the name of the person proposing the discussion. On this list there were two items, one listed to the Mayor herself and one to Tim Byrne, and that's when I really started paying attention. The

Mayor's Motion was for the Council to approve and adopt the revised arrangements for the upcoming local elections. I had never thought about the need for such a document, though now it made sense to have one, and I had certainly never read one, but it appeared that most of these people had, and the Motion passed without discussion.

Finally, the mayor nodded at Tim and said questioningly,

'Councillor Byrne, you have a Motion.'

Tim stayed in his seat, while his sparkling smile took in the whole company, and I was aware of a sense of real expectancy: clearly, there were some around this giant table who knew what was coming.

'Madam Mayor,' he began to a now-silent room, 'I would like to propose that this Council recognises the Guardians as a new political party, prior to the local elections.'

And he looked directly at me with a hint of triumph in his smile, as if to say 'There. I've done it'.

There was a pause, followed by some muttering, until the Mayor spoke,

'I've never heard of them,' she said, and I noticed a little sourness in her voice. She was obviously not telling the truth here – she had heard of them, knew who they were. 'Why do we need to recognise a party that doesn't exist?'

Tim rose this time, in a kind of magnificent calm,

'With your permission, Madam Mayor, there will be some members here who will be standing under their banner at the next elections. If their name is to appear on ballot papers they must be recognised.'

'Who?' asked the Mayor sharply. 'Who, that is, apart from you, Mr Byrne?'

So I was right – she had known about them already.

Tim's smile didn't waver as he looked around the table.

'Ladies,' he said, an invitation in his voice. 'Gentlemen?'

After the briefest pause, six Councillors, including John Placide and the distracted deputy head, stood in harmony and solidarity, smiling as broadly (smugly?) as Tim. This had clearly been

planned, rehearsed even, and was beginning to look like some sort of coup. I watched for the varying reactions, to find some of those who had not stood with the new group smiling in congratulation or bemusement, while a couple of those still sitting were clearly put out, even outraged, like the Mayor, who broke the silence with, 'All of you? So, this is what you've been plotting.'
'Plotting, Madam Mayor?' said Tim in deliberately feigned innocence, the radiant smile undimmed: he was really good at unsettling people. 'We all want to keep doing the jobs we've been doing,' the other six nodding in agreement, 'just as a group instead of a bunch of individuals. Makes us stronger, don't you think?'
'But you already belong to a party,' the Mayor's protests already sounding hollow, 'apart from you, of course, Mr Byrne.'
'Well, now I do, Madam Mayor. And we'd be grateful if you would recognise us.'
And he sat then, knowing the Mayor would have no choice now but to concede the vote. The rest of his new group sat as he did and we all waited expectantly, the reporter leaning forward, pencil poised, until I thought he might fall over the front wall of the gallery.
'Very well, then,' said the distinctly uncomfortable Ms Patel, 'by show of hands please indicate those here who would recognise this group as an official political party.'
Before the hands could rise Tim interrupted,
'We're called the Guardians.'
There was a pause, and I am sure I saw Ms Patel grind her teeth.
'Very well, I shall ask again,' she was speaking more quietly now. 'Please raise your hands all those in favour of recognising the Guardians as an official political party in Ordnage.'
Tim interrupted again, and I thought Ms Patel was actually going to lose her temper.
'Not just in Ordnage, Madam Mayor.'
'Very well.' She was exasperated now and was almost hissing. 'Please raise your hands all those who would recognise the Guardians as an official political party.'
She stopped there this time, and glanced at Tim to see if that was

good enough. He gave her a gracious nod and raised his hand, fist clenched. The others followed, and when I looked to make a quick count it was only the Mayor and two others whose hands were not up.

'Those against,' she muttered redundantly, as she raised her hand, but the muted cheering, the congratulations, even a few expletives, told her all she needed to know.

The reporter was scribbling frantically as the meeting broke up and I made my way downstairs to the main chamber to congratulate Tim and the others. I was so glad I had chosen this evening to come to my first meeting – it was truly exciting. As I entered the room I could see Tim's head was down as he was looking at his phone, but I made my way across to him and waited for him to look up. When he saw me he smiled again (wow, that was an engaging grin) and indicated his phone,

'Just letting Russell know,' he said, even though I hadn't asked. 'Glad you came?'

'Wow,' I said, 'just wow. Are they always as tense as that?'

He laughed, 'Never!'

'The Mayor seemed a bit put out,' I commented.

He dismissed the idea with, 'She'll get over it. Has no choice now, does she?'

And I'm sure I detected a hint of self-satisfaction. I think he had enjoyed the little battle of wills that I had just witnessed. Before he could get to the door the reporter stopped him,

'Can I have a word, Tim?'

Now it was the reporter's turn to receive the dazzling smile.

'Ah, Pete, glad you're here. Can we meet soon? Maybe tomorrow.'

'OK, shall I come to you?' He acquiesced without protest, gave no indication that he felt brushed off. Even the press was under his spell, it seemed. And Tim continued before the reporter could ask him anything else,

'Anyone for the George?' Louder now, to include the room. 'Pete? Join us for pint?'

'Thanks, Tim,' said the reporter, 'but I have to file. This is real

news, and you know that's hen's teeth around here.'
They laughed together before the reporter made his way out.

There was quite a little crowd walking to the pub this time – the four of us from the last time, all the newly-recognised Guardian group, and a couple of extras; the pace was brisk and there was a lot of excited chattering all the way. There was no match on tonight, so there was plenty of space in the saloon, and we made our way to the largest table in the corner, with people dragging stools and chairs over to make us one group.
'I think the first round's on you, then, Tim,' said John.
'Already on its way,' he said as the barman approached with a tray full of glasses and two bottles of wine. Again, he had been prepared. The wine wasn't champagne but the mood was. I didn't really join in with the conversation – not only was I still the outsider for now in a well-established group, but much of what they talked about came from that shared history, and I was not a part of that yet. We began with a toast, of course, 'to the Guardians', before there was the usual splintering into smaller conversations and sub-groups. People began to leave quite soon, one or two at a time, until it was just the Guardian seven and me, drinking our way towards closing time.

As the first bell went the distracted deputy head asked Tim,
'So what's next, boss?'
'Not tonight, Alice.' I was relieved to hear someone call her by her name, so now I could stop calling her by her job title. 'Tonight's just for celebration. The work starts next week. Monday OK for everybody?'
There were nods around the table.
'My place, 7 o'clock?'
More nods.
'We'll start with nominations, then have a look at the manifesto. OK?'
There were murmurs of agreement as I saw my chance. I reached into my bag and produced the smart little documents I had

conjured at work. With some pride I spread them out on the table and said,
'Talking of the manifesto, I put these together. Just some examples.'
Then I sat back, waiting for their comment.
I suppose I was hoping, probably unreasonably, for some praise, or at least constructive criticism, for the thought I had given them if not for the content. I wasn't prepared for the dismissive and slightly hostile,
'We've got the professionals working on those,' from Alice.
Nobody even picked one up, and I thought I detected a little muted sniggering from a couple of the others at the table. I was really embarrassed now, and was immediately grateful when Tim made an attempt to rescue my dignity, as he patted the mauve one with, 'It's a start. Thanks, Kelly,' though it wasn't my imagination that his head was tipped slightly to one side, so I still felt patronised.
I shuffled all the bits of paper together, then picked up my coat and bag and stood up, muttering,
'I'd better get off home.'
I just wanted to be away from these people who had made me feel ridiculous. Though I could see, even from this close, that I had probably done it to myself. What was I thinking, trying to set myself up as some great designer of political materials? But I knew it wasn't some high political ideal I was trying to address, nor a whole party I was trying to impress. As I started to move away from the table, head down, I felt that hand on my arm.
'Give me a minute, Kelly. I'll take you home.'
Then I was seriously conflicted. Not only did I not fancy the bus journey on my own after dark, but I really wanted to be close to him, even if it was only for 20 minutes in the car. Actually I wanted to cry.
'I'll wait outside.'
I heard the final bell as I stood in the doorway of the pub, hoping he came out before the others passed me. I was in luck. The others were with him, but he took my arm and led me away before I had to think of something to say to them. I didn't know if I would be

able to face any of them ever again.

There were no words between us until we were almost back to the Town Hall car park.
'Thanks for that, Kelly,' he began, but I cut him off.
'Please don't,' I said tearfully. 'I feel like an idiot.'
He stopped walking then and turned me to face him.
'Why? Because you made an effort? Because you tried to do something nice for me? Stop it. I said thank you, and I meant it.'
'It was amateurish nonsense, and I should have seen that for myself.'
'Now you're fishing,' he said, and gave a little laugh.
It was infectious as always and I found myself beginning to smile along with him.
'I guess I'm just taking myself too seriously,' I almost whispered.
'Something like that,' he said. 'Now, come on, let's get you home. It's cold out here.'

During the journey we went over the evening a little, the bit before my humiliation in the pub, that is, and it felt as if we already had a tacit agreement never to mention that again. I told him again how tense it had been for those of us observing the proceedings, and made him laugh with the little vision of the reporter hanging dangerously, and almost literally, on their every word. By the time we reached my flat I was feeling much better and I invited him in for coffee. For 'coffee'.
'If you're sure,' he said. 'It's a bit late for a school night,' and we both acknowledged his reference to my small joke with a grin.
'Oh, no,' I said with feigned nonchalance, 'I always need to wind down a bit when I've been out. Couldn't go to bed yet.'
'OK, then, coffee it is. I'm assuming you have decaf at this time of night,' and he laughed.

I put the kettle on and set up the cups while he stood watching me from the other side of the kitchen. Before I could ask he said, 'Milk, no sugar, please,' so I didn't even look up while we continued

with pointless small talk. (I think I said something about how differently everybody likes their coffee, and how I always make it at work – just filling silence.) As I turned, a steaming mug in each hand, he was right in front of me, looking me squarely in the eye.
'Blimey, you're a ninja!' I said. 'You were over there...'
'And now I'm over here. Right here. Is that OK?'
He was speaking very softly, almost as if there were somebody else in the room, and he didn't want them to hear.
I just nodded. Hell, yes, it was more than OK.
He moved forward, so that I had to hold the mugs out sideways to let him in, finding myself deliciously trapped. He brushed his lips on mine, then leant back just a little.
'Is this OK?
I nodded again, already amused at how quickly I had lost the power of speech, and his face was on mine, hungry and demanding. Of course I responded, boiling coffee notwithstanding. Eventually he pulled away, but not before whispering into my ear,
'Can we dispense with the coffee, Kelly? I'd rather have you. I'm sorry, but I just do. Is that OK with you?'
I suppose it should have been sleazy, but I didn't see it that way at all: he had taken a risk here, making himself vulnerable with such an invitation out of the blue, as it were. I should have been horrified, but in fact I found it oh, so inviting. I wasted no effort on fake denials or pretence – I had probably wanted him from the moment I first saw him – but just turned back to put the cups down.
'Not in here,' I said, and led him into my bedroom.

That first time was everything it should have been, the way everybody's first time should be – patient, tender, committed. Sex with Geoff had always been a little traditional, even functional, I now realised, more satisfying in a physical sense than emotionally. We only ever undressed ourselves, made love under the covers when the day was finished, no surprises and little variety. So this was a whole new way for me: we undressed each other carefully, Tim guiding my hands gently to what he wanted me to do, slowing me down, teasing me just enough, kissing me in places I had never been kissed before, and yes, looking after me, though I'm sure nobody would have interpreted it in a political sense! At one point I tried to say something encouraging, but he stilled me with a soft 'shh', fingers on my lips, then kissed me again. It wasn't only in the council chamber that he was confident. There was no background music, no sound beyond our own, and it was, without doubt, the most intense experience I had ever had up until that moment, and I didn't want it to stop.

It was almost an hour later when Tim lifted himself up from the bed and said he had to leave now. I pouted like a small child and said,
'Do you have to? You can stay if you want to.'
'I can't, Kelly, I'm sorry. Think how it would look.'
'No-one would know.'
'We would,' he said. A man with principles!
'I've got a spare toothbrush...'
He laughed gently then, but still kept putting his clothes on.
'But look what you're leaving behind,' I said, sitting up on the edge of the bed and dangling my breasts at him. I would have stood and pressed myself against him, anything to keep him here, but I wasn't sure my legs would support me right now.
'Very tempting,' he grinned as he buttoned his shirt, 'but I really can't. I'm sure I could come another time, though, if that's OK with you.'
'Do you want a key?' - my feeble attempt at being seductive.
'Should I come to your meeting on Monday?'
I needed something concrete to make sure we would see each other again, and soon.
'Not Monday,' he said, and I could feel him slipping back into the impeccable professional I had first met. 'That's for the new party members, and we have a lot of business to get through. I'm sorry, Kelly. Life's going to be a bit frantic between now and the elections. I'll call you.'

This sounded too much like a brush-off, and I didn't like it at all, so I let myself (not to mention the sisterhood) down with,
'But when will I see you again?' Pathetic. I'd be begging him next. I saw him flinch, just the merest pause, and then the mask came back into place.
'Will you still volunteer for us?'
'Of course. You tell me when and where and I'll be there.' I could hardly back out now.
'Good, good,' he said distractedly, and his thought processes were almost visible. Was he thinking about how he could see me again, or worse, about how he could avoid it?
'I'll be calling a meeting for all the volunteers in a week or so. I'll make sure you get the details.'
Really? Just another volunteer? Was that it? Was that all I was? Was this how he made all his political conversions?
'OK, thanks,' I said as casually as I could manage, and it was at just the moment I had given up that he salvaged the whole mess: dressed now, he pulled me up off the bed and towards him with both arms around me. He kissed me warmly, then leant back as if looking at me for the first time, and said,
'You were wonderful. You know I'll be back. How could I not?'

I didn't call Beth straight away, though I'm not sure why. It certainly wasn't out of any consideration for her: though I'm sure she would have been asleep by now, we had been on 24-hour call for each other since we were about 16, so if I had really wanted to speak to her I could have done so without guilt or censure. It could have been that I wanted to hug this to myself for a while before sharing it, despite our usual habit of sharing every secret and detail. But more likely it was the slight inkling that what had just happened wasn't right somehow. I couldn't quite grasp how yet, and I needed to process it for myself before I ran it through the steely and objective scrutiny of Ms Conscience, currently in a hotel somewhere in Newcastle. Maybe I would talk to her about it when she came home at the weekend. I didn't.

I was delighted, though, when Tim turned up at my flat just after 10 o'clock on the following Monday evening. I was already slopping about the house in my pyjamas, feeling a bit morose because he hadn't called, drinking hot chocolate for comfort, and pretending to read. When the doorbell rang I jumped, knowing somehow that it was him, though that may have been more wishing than premonition. I ran downstairs to open the door, and greeted him with the sort of uninhibited hug usually reserved for someone coming home from war. We went upstairs and pretended to make coffee while he chattered excitedly about the progress they had made at their meeting and I just wanted him to get his clothes off. The coffee was ignored again as I got my way.

And that became the pattern of my life for the next few weeks: he got busier and busier with meetings and hustings, all sorts of campaigning and organisation, while I sat at home every evening, hoping he would come and share his successes with me, and yes, make love to me. I felt myself craving him like chocolate, and he accepted the other key, Geoff's key, within a fortnight. I did join the volunteer group, even registered as a party member, though if I were being honest with myself, it was more about hoping to see him, spend a little time in the same room as him, than doing my bit for the elections. I even delivered leaflets some evenings on my way home from work and at weekends, but any political fervour I may have felt when I began all this had worn off quickly, subsumed under the entirely personal.

Whenever he did come to me at the end of the evening, once or twice a week, I was grateful, and desperate to be welcoming and seductive so he wouldn't stop coming. Just once I suggested I was a bit tired for sex, though in truth I think it was more a case of testing the balance of the relationship – would he stay this time, maybe even hug me till I was asleep? Could we actually just have a conversation (and not a political one!)? Did we have a relationship at all beyond sex?

Tim's response to that was dismissive to say the least:
'You know you'll love it once we get going,' as he pulled me towards him and carried on almost as if I wasn't there. I was disappointed, naturally, but was so soon swept up in the blur of joy at what he could do to me, how he made me feel, that I convinced myself I was happy with whatever he was prepared to give me, and I hadn't really meant it when I said I was too tired – I wanted him to see through my ruse and persuade me. It was all over much more quickly than usual – my fault for saying I was tired I suppose - and I assumed he was trying to make me feel better when he said, 'There, that didn't take too long, did it?'
Like he was doing me a favour.

It was only later, much later, that I realised how coercive his behaviour was. It was as if I had relinquished my right to choice. Oh, I knew it was all unhealthy, (and Beth, when I finally told her, made no attempt at diplomacy and told me I was an idiot to let him dictate the rules) and I was probably inflicting lasting damage on my self-esteem, but I told myself I was a willing participant in whatever this relationship was, who wasn't being used, and was prepared to accept the crumbs. It was a month or so before the elections when we had 'the' conversation. After yet another fleeting late-night visit I made the tentative suggestion that we could actually go out together some time, just to a pub or even for a walk.
'Wouldn't it be nice to do something normal, together?' I pouted disingenuously.
I recognised my error instantly as I watched the shutters come down as he pulled his shirt over his head.
His dismissal was swift: 'You know how busy I am'.
I tried to rescue it with, 'I feel as if I'm being hidden.' It sounded pathetic even to me. I think I was trying to turn this into a real debate about the nature of our relationship, but he was having none of it.
'I'm sorry you feel like that. I thought we were just enjoying each other's company.'

'We are,' I was rather too emphatic now. 'But wouldn't you like to take a night off, do something frivolous for a change, just once?'

'I don't have time for frivolous things right now. I have an election to win.'

I could feel an unfamiliar anger in his tone and instinctively backed off.

'I know, I know,' I tried to soothe him. 'I just thought it would be nice.'

I didn't question my own capitulation. I was turning into (had already become?) the sort of woman I would have sneered at so recently. I wonder what Geoff would say if he could see this version of me.

His anger seemed to have dissipated as soon as it had come. Perhaps he wasn't really cross at all; perhaps it was just my imagination.

'You know how things are, Kelly. That was never part of the deal.'

What deal? We had never discussed the terms of this relationship. Is this how he saw us for ever - late night visits, all on his terms, no public acknowledgement, no commitment? I didn't ask because I didn't want to hear his answer.

And then the coup de grace, 'Perhaps you would rather I didn't come at all.'

I laughed then, a hasty, nervous, too-loud cackle.

'Of course not. Don't be silly.'

That was the end of any discussion, and I guess we both now recognised where we stood.

And that was another conversation I didn't tell Beth about.

5.

The end of this arrangement coincided, or should I say came crashing down, with the council elections. I had been building them up in my mind, imagining that once they were over he would have the time to spend with me, and we could develop a real relationship the way it was meant to be, or at least how I pictured it. It was all a bit hearts and flowers, to be honest, most unlike my previous collected self. (I conveniently ignored any comparisons with the years I had spent bobbing along somewhat aimlessly with Geoff.) For those last couple of weeks I became the most enthusiastic party member they had, ready and available to do any job they needed me for, though none of them knew my reasons were far less altruistic than I assumed theirs were. I had long since been forgiven for my naïve attempts at amateur design, and contented myself with answering phones and trudging the streets.

Just a few days before the polls we were all at yet another meeting in the back room at John's restaurant when Tim asked the room,
'So who is coming to the count?'
Now I had already looked up what all this meant – I didn't ever again want to appear uninformed or stupid by being floored by jargon or specialist vocabulary – so I knew this was the evening of the election, when anybody was welcome to go to the town hall and sit in as observers to the counting of the ballots. It all sounded more than a bit dull, to be honest, but if it meant spending time with Tim, and being there to congratulate him when he won (we were all confident this was a done deal) then I was most certainly in. I put my hand up, along with several of the others, including Alice, and Tim himself, of course. It was only later I realised that

they would all be there as candidates, and I was the only one who was a mere member. In the intervening weeks more and more of the Council had been mesmerised by Tim's magnetism, or perhaps had been persuaded by the power and vision of his arguments and policies, and had switched parties in time to stand as Guardians. If they all won in their various wards then they would be the majority party. Ms Patel and her shrinking faithful cohort were not at all pleased! I suppose I should have been excited, if I had thought of the evening as being in at the birth of a new movement, but I was far more interested in the notion that Tim would no longer be too busy for me.

I had taken the day following the election off work, so I would be able to stay at the count as late as necessary, and even managed to slip off home early 'to make sure I get my vote in'. I had changed out of my work clothes and was thinking about maybe splashing out on a cab to the town hall, when I heard the key in the front door. That could be only one person, and I found myself instantly thrilled that he had chosen to share his excitement with me, maybe even travel with me – public at last!
How disappointed I was to be. He opened with,
'What a night this is going to be!' Before I could concur he grabbed me and pushed me towards the bed.
'Wish me luck in the way you know best,' he teased, and those twinkly eyes were all I could see. I didn't have time to protest (even if I had wanted to) and was soon caught up in the fastest and fiercest sex I had experienced to date. His hands and mouth were everywhere, only the essential bits of clothing were removed, and I barely registered which way was up before he was heading for the door.
'Wait!' I said, quite querulously, pulling at my underwear. 'We can go together.'
He laughed then, and it wasn't kind.
'I don't think so, Kelly,' and the twinkle was still there, just with an edge of cruelty. 'You'll be wanting a shower now, won't you?'
'Well, yes, I guess,' I tried, 'but we can still go together, if you could

wait.'

'Not going to happen, sweetie. I need to be there. And you need to change.'

It took a moment to register what he was suggesting. I was really slow these days.

'But I am changed,' I said feebly. 'What's wrong with it?'

It was jeans and a jumper. How could he possibly be objecting to jeans and a jumper? And what did it matter what I was wearing?

'Well, if you think it's alright,' he said, and I was sure I noted just a tiny note of sneering. 'Who am I to tell you what to wear?'

The tone was unmistakeable this time: that was exactly what he was doing – trying to direct my clothing. Even Geoff would never have tried to tell me what to wear. And for the first time since I had met him little shoots of doubt actually penetrated the fog of my devotion. Before I could frame a response, though, he left with,

'I'll see you there, then. It's going to be a great night.'

I stood for a while after he had gone, looking at myself in the bedroom mirror. I wondered what he saw when he looked at me. Oh, I don't mean 'what did he see in me?' I knew now, or at least suspected what he saw in me, what use I was to him, and it wasn't comfortable reflection. Was I really just a casual shag? This was what Beth had been trying to persuade me to see all along.

My next decision was crucial. Never had what I chose to wear assumed such significance. I had always floated comfortably between professional dress and leisure-wear, barely thought about formal clothes or the right clothes for shopping – I just wore them all easily, never thought about them as any kind of badge. And it had been many years since anybody had decided for me what I should wear. It would have been my mum, I suppose, when I was little, but I don't remember her doing it even then. But now, did I change as he had suggested, dress up to please him, or should I go with my original choice? After a fleeting image of myself wearing just a coat with nothing underneath (how would you like that, Mr Self-Important?) I decided to keep the jeans and add a shirt rather than the casual sweater, though I didn't refresh my makeup. Yes, I was compromising as usual.

I didn't need to be at the town hall until after the polls closed at 10 o'clock, so I flicked on the television, to fill the silence as much as anything. This was unusual for me – I was definitely a radio fan when it came to giving myself a bit of undemanding company in the house – but it felt like fate when I found myself staring at Tim Byrne's twinkly smile coming at me out of the screen. My first ludicrous thought was that I had been transported into a parallel universe, where my feelings were being projected at me, or I was being taken over by some outside influence. But then I listened to the article on our regional network, and wondered whose stroke of genius had managed to get Tim and his crew some highly favourable publicity.

'…the people of Ordnage have a different choice today…' intoned the shiny presenter, '…the new Guardian party.'

She continued with a whistlestop outline of their growth locally, with a nod to the possibility of a wider network, mentioned that intoxicating strapline 'we'll look after you', and finished with an attempt at an interview with the man himself. Someone shoved a microphone at him and asked what he thought his chances were in the elections, and he smiled his warmest and most inclusive smile as he said,

'Well, I don't want to be seen to try and influence people's votes at this late stage, but we mean what we say.'

He finished with a warm 'thank you' and was seen disappearing into an imposing-looking granite building (the Town Hall, maybe), framed by a clear night sky. He radiated charisma, even in this snippet, and the camera loved him.

I was shocked. This had clearly not been filmed today – we were still in daylight – and I couldn't imagine it was anything that had taken him by surprise, so why had he not told me about it? This was more than a coup, a reason to celebrate, surely. This was the beginning of him climbing onto a much wider stage. It looked as if he were being taken seriously, certainly seriously enough to be

mentioned on the local news. And yet he hadn't told me. Before I could drive myself crazy with trying to work out why not I phoned Beth. I didn't even say hello before blurting out excitedly,
'Tim was just on the telly.'
As usual, Beth was cool and measured and made me pause when she said,
'Hello to you, too. Yes, my day was busy, but I managed to get a lot done. No, I haven't eaten yet. Yes, Elvis is fine, thank you. How are you?'
I ignored her attempts at sardonic humour and just carried on as if she hadn't spoken.
'They had an article on the local news. They interviewed him and everything.'
I knew she wouldn't have seen the article herself as she was a long way from home again this week, so wouldn't have access to the local channels.
'He's really going somewhere, Beth. He's going to win this, and then, who knows?'
As I hung up I failed to question myself again – why was I sharing only the celebrations with my dearest friend these days? Yet again, I didn't mention what had happened just a short time ago - the flying visit, the hasty sex, the telling me what to wear. The unmistakeable dismissal. I wasn't sorry that Beth didn't have time to stay on the phone for very long.

I don't know why but I thought I'd go early and soak up some atmosphere, see what was happening. I wasn't kidding myself – I was going to see Tim, see how he was after our strange little encounter earlier. I turned off the television, grabbed my jacket and headed for the bus.

The town hall was seething. I tried to be near Tim, but he barely said hello, certainly didn't acknowledge me more than anybody else there. He was 'working the room', moving between groups, drawing people in, shaking a lot of hands, and being the eager puppy I had first seen all those months ago. I had never managed to become one of what I thought of as his inner circle, and now felt a bit abandoned. Even the rest of the Guardians seemed to be too involved to give me more than a cursory and somewhat impersonal hello. I was glad to see there were plenty of others like me, people who didn't seem to belong to any particular group. Then, as the ballot boxes arrived, there was a definite shift in the atmosphere, as everybody moved away from the centre of the room to allow the boxes to be placed on the runway of tables that ran the length of the main chamber. The ballot-counters were all in their places, with the Returning Officer issuing final instructions and making sure everybody and everything were where they should be.

Boredom set in fairly quickly – watching bits of paper being tipped out of boxes and put into piles was not an absorbing spectator event, and I was glad to find myself next to Pete, the local reporter, when he began chatting to me. He had no idea who I was, of course, but clearly remembered seeing me at meetings, and was at least a friendly face.
'Pete Compton,' he said, offering his hand. 'With the Chronicle. I think we've met before.'
'Kelly Arben. I've been to a few meetings.'
'That'll be where I've seen you. Vested interest or just curiosity?'
Now that was an interesting question. One I wasn't sure how to answer, so I just laughed a little.
'It's not very exciting, is it?' I said.
'It'll warm up later,' he laughed with me. 'Do you fancy a coffee while we wait for it to get going?'
Actually, I did, and the thought of getting out of here for a while was appealing, so we made our way into the large anteroom that had been commandeered as a makeshift canteen for the evening. I managed to find us a table, squashed into a corner by the door, as he went to the urns and came back with a couple of large paper cups with lids.
'I didn't know if you wanted a biscuit or something, so I got these,' and he pulled a muffin from each coat pocket and put them down

with the coffees while he settled onto the chair beside me. 'I think we're going to need the energy if we're staying till the end.'

'And will you be staying?' I asked, more for something to say than out of genuine interest. My real interest in the evening lay elsewhere.

'No choice,' he muttered through a mouthful of blueberry muffin. 'It's my job.'

'Any idea how long it's likely to go on for?' I asked, actually wanting to hear his answer. I was trying not to be excited about what might happen later.

'Oh, this lot are usually pretty efficient,' he said warmly. 'We should be out of here by about 3. 2 if we're lucky.'

I was really glad I had taken the next day off work!

I assume his job made him easy to be with, and I found myself liking him. He was probably a couple of years older than me, dark and bearded, and a little overweight (I wasn't surprised when I later discovered he had been called Pudgy Pete at school), but was unlike the stereotype of a local reporter – not only was he smartly dressed in a sober suit and wore an expensive watch, but I didn't find myself being wary of every word I said to him. I instinctively trusted him.

On this occasion our superficial conversation lasted only as long as the coffee, and Pete stood and dusted a crumb off his coat.

'I'd better get back in there,' he said. 'I don't want to miss anything, do I?' and the slight lift of one eyebrow told me he knew he was being ironic.

I waved acknowledgement and said I'd see him later.

I popped back into the coffee-room several times during the count, mostly to break up the tedium, and, of course, then had to go and find a ladies more than once. I was tempted to pull up my Kindle on my phone and find a quiet corner to sit and read a book, but I found a growing interest in the anthropology of the occasion. (Is anthropology the same as people-watching?) All the 'types' were here – professionals and those with a casual interest, the fussy and the calm, the experienced and the youthful enthusiasts, though what I found particularly fascinating was the way groups were made, broken up, re-made. What I watched mostly, though, was Tim, already the consummate politician. He had a word, a smile, a comment for everybody, and there was no doubting the expectation in his manner – he already wore the winner's mantle.

Finally, there was another shift in the atmosphere in the chamber, and it became clear the count was completed. All the candidates shuffled onto the stage at the end of the room, while the Returning Officer tapped the microphone at the front, and the rest of us jostled for space on the floor around the tellers, most of whom stayed in their seats and looked shattered. I noticed Pete Compton was on the side of the platform, presumably so he could note down the details of the results without having to compete for space in the bull-pen the rest of us had to make do with. As the Returning Officer ran through the formalities and a lot of numbers I tried to catch Tim's eye, to signal my support. But it was if I no longer existed. He stood with the rest of the candidate group – Audrey and Alice, John and Ashraf, plus a few others I recognised as candidates by their rosettes, and a couple of people I had never seen before: there was a Tim-clone in a smart suit, whom I considered might be his brother, they looked so alike; there was a very well-groomed young woman at his shoulder, in a long camel coat, casually open to show some very expensive silk underneath. We had exchanged no more than a few awkward words during the whole evening, and he didn't appear to be seeking me out as I had hoped he would. The only person whose eye I caught was Pete's, and there was no meaning in the glance. I tried to take in all the figures I was hearing, but I could barely even take in who had won what – it was just one name I was listening for.

And then it came. I was subsumed in the cheering and thunderous applause when it became clear that Tim and his fellow Guardians had enacted the coup they had intended – they were now the ruling party, and he was their undisputed leader. The prolonged whooping and air-punching were hypnotic and I couldn't help but be swept up in their triumph, until I found myself 'shushing' along with everybody else as Tim stepped forward to take the mic. I was sure I noticed tears in his eyes as he began,

'I am honoured that the people of this great town have chosen us to represent their interests, to lead and support them into their futures.'

Every sentence provoked another round of cheering. He had already become the local hero.

'But this is not just me, not even just the party team to thank for our success. There have been a lot of individuals who have put in a lot of hours and effort, and I would like to take this opportunity to thank them all.'

Was this going to be my moment? Please.

'First, there are all our party workers, who have trodden the streets, managed a lot of leafleting and getting the message out there.'

Well, that was me certainly, but he didn't go on to single out any of us individually, so maybe he was saving me for special mention.

'There are those who have lent us space – John -' and here he brought John Placide forward to share the front of the stage with him – 'Des –' I recognised the landlord of the George.

'Thank you also to my valiant opponents, who have fought this election with dignity and fairness, and I look forward to continuing to serve on the Council with some of them as colleagues.'

At this I watched Chadni Patel move to the side of the stage and disappear into the wings, her face a mask of controlled misery. She had lost her seat and was clearly unhappy about it.

'But most of all, I couldn't have done this without the love and support of my own family.'

Was I going to be included amongst a list of his nearest and dearest? I was poised to step forward into his limelight when I heard what came next.

'Please say thank you with me to my beautiful fiancée. Come and join me, please, Shannon.'

And the camel coat and silk was being kissed publicly, as the rest of the stage party closed around them.

There was a lot of movement then – people leaving, others trying to get up to join in the celebrations, officials beginning the clearing-up and putting away – but I did not, could not join in. I heard and saw the scene as if I were no longer part of it, the chaos of fast-moving water in my ears, blurring around me, trying to focus on what I was seeing through the instant tears. I knew, then, what it meant to be truly beside oneself – I felt dissociated from this new reality. All the times Tim had come to me, all the time I had invested in him, all of it a lie, deliberate deception. So this was what he had meant by 'the deal'. I managed to collect myself enough to get to the ladies I was glad I had found earlier, where I was hideously and noisily sick, and it wasn't because of the muffin. I didn't know if there was anybody else in there, and I didn't care. As soon as I could I fled then, out of the building, away from my terrifying humiliation, and just kept walking, fast. I couldn't get on a bus in this state, wasn't even sure any more where the bus stops were, I just wanted to be away from there, away from him. If I were being honest, it was myself I needed to be away from. What an idiot I had been! No matter how badly I felt he had behaved, what sort of snake I thought he was, I couldn't avoid the conclusion that I had colluded in whatever the relationship, such as it was, had evolved into. I hadn't challenged him once, had made no demands in my own interest.

I tried to bring my woeful snivelling under control, but I knew I wasn't ready for rational thought and reflection, so I just kept walking, both to put distance between him and myself, and to try and raise some endorphins with brisk exercise. I was actually doing quite well with all that until it started to rain. It felt like a personal attack when the very cloud that was hovering over my head was the one to breach its celestial boundaries, and I was drenched almost instantly. It felt like a final humiliation, and I gave up the fight for self-control. I stopped on the pavement and howled my rage in incoherent bellowing.

It was at exactly that moment that a car pulled up beside me and opened the passenger door.
'Kelly?' said a voice from the dark interior.
My first thought was, of course, that it was Tim coming to find me, apologise, make me safe, and I was already searching for the right (caustic?) response when the voice continued,
'Get in! You're soaked.'
I bent down to deliver some pithy dismissal only to see that the driver was Pete Compton.
'But your seats...' I began to protest.
'They're only plastic. Just get in.'
So I did, relieved that I didn't have to find the wherewithal to cope with arguing with Tim for now.
'What on earth are you doing?' he continued as I slammed the door. 'Hardly the best weather for a nice walk home on your own at three o'clock in the morning.'
I was instantly defensive, and in no mood for repartee or conviviality.
'I don't need your censure. Are you offering me a lift or not?'
'Of course I am,' and he smiled generously. 'Where to, Ma'am?'
I was immediately sorry for snapping at him. He didn't know the background, could have no idea of the depths of my embarrassment and self-loathing right now.
I looked around and was surprised to find I knew where I was, about halfway home. I had run out with no plan or direction in my mind; I guess I had just headed for home instinctively. I directed him from there, but not another word passed between us until we were outside my house, where I muttered my thanks and started to open the door. Before I could make my escape he spoke again,
'Look, are you alright?'
I laughed, though there was no amusement in it.
'I saw you leave.'
How marvellous – a witness to my humiliation.

'Do I look alright?' Sarky.
'Well,' he said thoughtfully, 'I don't know you well, but you don't look exactly tiptop.'
I thought, just for a moment, of telling him the whole wretched story, but then I remembered what he did for a living, and thought better of laying my soul bare to someone who had the platform to make me a fool in public as well as in private. In the end I went with the bland,
'I will be. I guess I'm just wet and cold.'
He handed me his card then.
'Well, if you're sure. You can always ring me.'
I was immediately and irrationally incensed again. Another macho arsehole trying to take advantage of a clearly vulnerable woman?
'Ring you? Why would I do that? Are you hitting on me?' and I was beginning to spit out the words.
He put his hands up defensively,
'Whoa, there, sister. My boyfriend really wouldn't like that.'
Oh, great, now I could feel stupid all over again.
'You're gay?'
'Yes,' he said noncommittally. 'Is that a problem for you?'
'Of course not,' I was flustered now. 'So why did you give me your card?'
'Reflex, I guess,' he said then. 'I hand them out like confetti. You never know when someone might have something they want to tell me.'
'I'm sorry,' I mumbled. 'And thank you,' as I finally got out of the car.
He waited until I was inside before he pulled away, as I paused behind the front door and just stood, trying to make some sense of my own idiocy and the ghastly events of the evening.

I could hear my mum's voice as an echo from my youth 'you'll get pneumonia' as I realised I was shivering, so I took off all my clothes (even my underwear was soaked) and left them on the landing where they dropped. I went to the bathroom and grabbed a towel, then into the kitchen and put on the kettle while I rubbed at my dripping hair. Hot chocolate was definitely prescribed – another of my mum's ready cures. Just as I was pouring the water into the mug I heard a sound that, frankly, and I'm not being melodramatic here, made my blood run cold – the key in the front door. There were only two people who had keys to my flat, and Beth was away, so it could be only one person. Before I could really register what might be happening Tim was standing in front of me, smiling impishly as if nothing had changed. I tried to angle the too-small towel to give myself some chance of dignity, but he snatched it out of my hand before I could cover myself at all.

'Ooh, ready for me right now, I see,' as he looked me up and down in a most unpleasant and proprietary way.
I have never felt more vulnerable; I realised I was actually afraid. How could he possibly think what he was doing was ok?
'Please give me back my towel,' was all I managed to put together, and in my confusion the towel was the most important thing, my only defence.
'You know you don't want it, not really,' and in another moment on the space-time continuum that would have been teasing and inviting. But right now it was just sleazy and frightening.
I saw he was pulling at his belt, and knew what was about to happen. I was fighting for equilibrium now, and I tried to pull a coherent thought, a plan for escape, from the swirling soup that was my brain: I knew I wouldn't be able to fight him – he would win, and I might get hurt; it would be pointless to try and race him to the phone or the front door; there was no one to hear if I started yelling. I went with the possibility of reason, usually my default setting.
'Please, Tim,' I started, 'I don't want this.'
'Sure you do,' he answered smugly, still pulling at his clothes, still smiling. 'You always want it.'
Did he see me as some kind of nymphomaniac? Or just a slut? Did he really not see that what I had wanted was him, just him?
'If I had known you had a girlfriend I would never have slept with

you.'

'What? Thinking of the sisterhood? It's a bit late for that.' He was really sneering now, though the tone of voice and the unwavering smile were a mismatch.

'I never lied to you, Kelly.'

Only by omission, you oily little man.

I found some anger then, and reached behind me to grab the mug I had just filled with boiling water, and launched it at him. But he had clearly anticipated an extreme reaction and stepped towards me and ducked sideways at the same time, so the mug smashed on the tiled wall behind him, covering every surface in my kitchen with boiling chocolate and lethal shards of porcelain. Almost before my arm was back at my side I felt the hideous thud as his hand connected with my face and my head snapped sideways.

'Really?' he sneered. 'Want it rough, do we?'

'No, please,' I tried again, my face already throbbing, but I knew it was feeble as I said it.

'Don't ever try that again, Kelly,' he was still sort of smiling, but dead-eyed now, like a great white, and while I really didn't feel myself to be in actual mortal danger, I knew I would come off worse if I didn't do as he said.

I made one last attempt at getting him to see reason:

'But you have a fiancée.'

'She doesn't appear to be here at the moment,' he grinned almost as if expecting me to join in with his little jape, and in place of the tender lover I had known such a short time before all I could see was a snarling bully.

'Come on, let's celebrate.'

I tried to say no, but before the word had even formed in my mouth he grabbed my arm and pulled me into my front room, ignoring my yelp as I stepped on some of the broken china. He pushed me down onto the floor, and stood over me while he cleared enough of his clothes to do what he needed to do.

'Ready for me, then?' he winked.

He actually winked at me, like I was in on the joke.

I tried to voice a protest again, but in reality I just felt paralysed.

I knew this was no longer about sex, if it ever had been, but power, and standing over me in obvious and childish physical domination was the metaphor. I guess enough of the soup had cleared to offer me the only practical solution – submit and get it over with. So that's what I did, even though it felt so wrong. Surely, women who didn't fight back were weak, or subconsciously asking for it. And a tiny treacherous little voice somewhere in the background told me I didn't really have the right to refuse – after all, I had been a willing participant so often and so recently.

When it was over I sat up and rather pointlessly pulled a cushion off the sofa to cover as much of myself as I could, while he just carried on dressing and smirking as if this had been just like all his other visits. I had always been proud of my body – well-proportioned, smooth skin – but now I just wanted to cover it up, keep it away from his leering glance. He didn't attempt small-talk, and I had nothing to say, so there was an eerie silence (I can't say it was awkward as I was the only one feeling uncomfortable) between us, punctuated only by the sounds of his clothes being replaced. As he moved towards the door I piped up, in a very small voice,
'Please leave your key,' and I wondered for the first time how many other keys he had in his pocket.
He turned towards me, the radiant and terrifying smile still unwavering.
'Why? How will I get in?'
I didn't know how to answer him. Surely, he couldn't possibly think we were going to carry on as before. But I managed to stay calm.
'I don't want you to come here again.'
He didn't pause even for a millisecond before,
'We both know that's not true, don't we?' and he leant forward, forcing a hand between the cushion and my skin, and tweaked my nipple painfully.
I think he really saw himself as some kind of irresistible celebrity.

'I told you tonight was going to be great, didn't I?'
And he was gone.

6.

In the three days before I had to go back to work I didn't leave my flat. Once I had, somewhat mechanically, cleared up the mess in the kitchen, and bathed and plastered my sore foot, I spent pretty much the whole time thinking, and my brain was not a comfortable place to inhabit! I had no doubt now that what had happened did indeed amount to rape. But to what extent could it be said that I had colluded? I didn't really fight, after all. If I reported it would anyone believe me? My history with this man was against me, all the other times I had been his willing partner taunting me from my consciousness. He was now a prominent local figure, with a growing profile and reputation, so who would doubt his version of events against mine?

And above all of this, thundering through my consciousness with all the subtlety of a charging rhino – my embarrassment and humiliation. Oh, not the humiliation of having submitted to rape, though that was bad enough – it was how I had allowed this man to seep into my soul, had welcomed his inattention, turned a blind eye to the realities of our 'relationship'. I was also saddened by the realisation that what had happened was not really a surprise. I had lost my real self in a welter of self-denial, had written off all the signs (of which there were many in all honesty) in hope and expectation, so there was no shock in hindsight that he had treated me with such disdain. That was what I had been asking for, not the rape, the humiliation.

Finally, early on Sunday evening, when I had at last achieved some kind of perspective on all that had happened, I rang Beth. She was only back for the weekend, so I deliberately left the call late so she wouldn't have hours (days?) to berate me. I should have known better. My perfect friend was everything I wanted her to be, all the support, all the sympathy, all the wisdom, and without even a hint of the 'I told you so' that would have been justified.

The call was short. Once I had told her the bare bones she cut me off with,

'I'm on my way.'

I tried to protest, without conviction (I guess I was really hoping she'd come),

'You don't have to…'

'Shut up, stupid girl. What would you be doing if situations were reversed?'

She arrived within 20 minutes, a couple of bottles of Merlot artfully balanced in one hand, and a carrier bag in the other. Before I could question the shopping she waved it at me and said,

'You haven't eaten, right?'

She was, of course, correct. I had barely thought of food all weekend, and realised I was starving. She tipped out a pile of snack-bags onto my coffee table and grabbed us a glass each, even before her coat was off.

'Right,' she said as we each took our first slug, 'tell me about the snake.'

I went right back to the beginning, and this time I left nothing out. She laughed when I told her about throwing the hot chocolate at him – 'good for you' – and insisted on checking my foot for damage, but other than that she let me talk uninterrupted for as long as it took. By the time I had finished the tale, including, finally, some honesty about how I was really feeling, I was relieved to find myself in tears. Maybe I was beginning to exorcise this spectre. I certainly felt better than I had in days. She was right – I am stupid: I should have told her before, kept her up with every step as it happened.

She sat back for a few seconds, then switched into the professional version of my friend. No wonder she was so successful at work – she saw straight to the heart of every issue instantly.

'Right. Plan of action, part 2.' And she came across to my sofa and gave me a firm and reassuring hug. 'And before you protest, I needed that as much as you did.' Bless her kind heart.

'Where was part one?' I said as she pulled back.

'You did that for yourself – you told me.'

'I'm sorry I didn't tell you before,' I found my lip quivering a bit. 'I know I should have.'

'Nonsense!' she dismissed my apology. 'You weren't ready to. I have no automatic right to your secrets, no one does. And you've told me now. So let's get on with it.'

'I don't know what to get on with.' I wasn't just being pathetic – after a whole weekend of reflection and attempted head-clearing I still genuinely didn't know how to move forward.

'That's what I'm here for,' she beamed. 'I can think clearly when you can't. You'd do the same for me in a heartbeat.'

She was right, although even her muddled thinking was usually more effective than mine at its clearest!

'Part three,' she carried on without a pause, 'tomorrow morning you're on to a locksmith. Change the lock.'

'I don't know any locksmiths.'

But she was prepared for all my dithering, woolly-headedness and backsliding. She pulled a business card out of her pocket and passed it over to me.

'This is Cliff. He does all the maintenance on our block. He'll be very happy to come and do that, and soon.'

'Great, thanks.'

'And don't let him in if he comes back.' She didn't mean Cliff.

'I won't.' I was quite confident of that. He had frightened me, and I knew I didn't want to invite that back in.

'Part 4 – report it.'

And this was the big stumbling-block for me. To report it meant going into detail about my own stupidity and blindness. I knew it would make me feel vulnerable, and it probably wouldn't result in anything other than more embarrassment. Beth saw my hesitation.

'You must, Kelly. It may be painful to acknowledge, but you're probably not the only one he's done this to. You owe it to the rest of us.'

I knew all that, but I wasn't confident. I talked her through all the reasoning I had done on my own.

'You see, it's just my word against his. Who's going to believe me?'

'I believe you.'

'Yes, but you love me. You know me. I don't think a stranger would. I'd just sound like a woman scorned.'

She was ready for that one, too.

'It needs to be on record somewhere. When he does it again, and he will, someone will find your story and realise there's more than just smoke on this particular fire.'

'Does it have to be the police?' I could feel an idea growing.

'Ideally it should be. They're the professionals. But what did you have in mind?'

A vision emerged then of my new friend, my knight on a white charger (OK, an old Vauxhall) from the night in question.

'What if I spoke to the local paper?' I suggested.

'Ooh,' she said, and I could see her working out the implications. 'They wouldn't be able to print it without some kind of proof or confirmation.'

'Would that matter?' I said, beginning to find some of my own clarity. 'It'll be evidence of a sort if anybody needs it later. Like you said – add to the smoke.'

'I'm liking your thinking.'

She didn't stay long after that. She had managed to make me laugh, asking me to picture Tim if the hot chocolate had landed as intended, and I guess that reassured both of us that I would be alright. She offered me her spare bed for as long as I needed it (I declined for both of us – she really did have to be up early, and I needed my own little cocoon for a while) then left the remnants of our little feast on the table.

The next morning at work I set to with a will. The first thing I had to do was get properly reinvolved with the business I was paid for; I knew I had let it all slide a bit, just going through the motions and doing the bare minimum while I was busy with Tim and the election, and I really owed them more than that: not only were they paying my salary (and a good one at that - Dorrett always joked that she'd bought my soul) but they were actually a decent bunch to be around. The atmosphere was always relaxed in the office, despite everybody working hard and genuinely pulling together in the way people do when they believe in what they are doing. We dealt in fancy goods – personalised and promotional stationery and other items – which may seem a trivial thing to be passionate about, but that's how it should be in a small but growing company like ours: everybody's role was crucial, and we all felt a loyalty to each other, so I was now feeling guilty that I had left all of them to pick up my slack. I realised I had been less than absorbed for a while now, and I was surprised I hadn't been 'taken aside'. I decided to pre-empt such embarrassment and went in to see Dorrett as soon as I saw she was free.

I opened with, 'Dorrett, I owe you an apology.'

'Do you indeed?' she said not at all unkindly.

'I know I've hardly been here, even when I've been here, if you see what I mean, and I'm sorry.'

She was sweetness itself.

'I did wonder.' So it hadn't just been my imagination, or rather my guilt. 'Is everything ok?'

So while I had been letting her down she had been worrying about me, bless her.

'It is now,' I said with confidence. I was sure I needed to throw myself back into work. 'It was this bloody election. I got, er, wrapped up in it for a while. Now it's over, I'm yours again.'

'I'm glad, Kelly. We've missed you.'

Had I really been that bad? Guiltier and guiltier.

'And thanks for popping in and letting me know.'

'It won't happen again.' I mentally crossed my fingers there, but I believed I had learned the lesson. Certainly I was sure I didn't ever want to repeat the embarrassment – I was worth more than that. From now on, I would compartmentalise my life properly.

She kissed my cheek as I left her office.

The kiss didn't go unnoticed by the rest of the team, and there was an almost audible sigh of relief around the room as people started throwing tasks my way and asking me questions as if nothing had ever happened. I really did work with some very nice people.

As soon as I found a moment, I pulled out the card Beth had left me and phoned Cliff. We made an appointment for him to come and change my lock on Wednesday evening. I assumed I'd be safe till then. Next, at lunchtime, I called Pete Compton. It went straight to voice, so I left a message for him to call me back, preferably this evening, as I might have a bit of a story for him. Beth's plans were shaping up.

The rest of the day was quite refreshing – I had forgotten how satisfying it is to be absorbed in a job you enjoy. I even went for a drink afterwards when Jenna suggested it, unusually for a Monday. I was grateful she had asked, actually. As my mum says, if you keep turning down invitations people will stop asking you, and I hadn't said yes in a long time. It turned out the toast for the evening was 'welcome back', aimed unequivocally at me. I really had been very self-centred for a while.

Pete rang me just after I got home, and I suggested we meet at my local, the Beggar's Arms. That way I could get myself something to eat while we talked. To be honest, I also wasn't ready to let any other unknown man into my house, gay or not. He agreed readily, and I could tell he was interested in what I might have to say. He was there when I arrived, and had already got in the first pint for each of us, a local brew – good choice, Pete. I was glad to have the Beggar's as my local. First, it was an attractive old barn of a place, with plenty of nooks for quiet conversation around an expanse of polished floorboards. The furniture was artfully mismatched, with a variety of soft and hard chairs that offered choice. There were large and smaller tables to suit any size party, and traditional games – darts, bar billiards, even skittles - each in their own space to keep them separate from the main floor. There was plenty of available parking (not that I ever needed it, living as close as I did), and, best of all, a really well-kept large garden for the warmer months. It had lanterns in the trees, scattered tables and benches, and was thoughtfully overgrown to offer a bit of shade and shelter to the smokers and fresh-air fiends. I had sat out here often in the weeks after Geoff, sometimes with Beth, often alone.

Pete declined dinner, but insisted on paying for mine 'it's all on expenses'. Win! We began with small talk, but as soon as my bangers and mash was in front of me, I got into my story.
'Ok,' I launched into it, 'you saw the state I was in last Thursday.'
He didn't comment, just made a 'duh' face at me. There was no malice in it and we both laughed a little.
'Well,' I continued, 'that was all about Tim Byrne.'
Pete showed no reaction other than attentiveness, just said 'Tell me more.'
So I told him the whole sordid story, culminating in the humiliation of election night, and the two visits that had left me feeling so used and stupid. I tried hard to keep to the facts, rather than embellish anything with my own slant, but it sounded dreadful any way you looked at it.
Pete made no comment during the narrative, and when I finished said nothing for longer than I would have expected. His thought processes were almost visible, as he sipped his pint and thought about what to do with all I had just revealed. For a brief moment I worried that he wasn't believing me, and started to say so, but he stopped me with a hand, then,
'I believe you, Kelly. Don't worry about that.'
I realised I was relieved at that. I didn't know how plausible this sorry saga would sound to anybody who didn't know me. And then it dawned on me – he wasn't surprised.
'Are there others?' I said tentatively, almost whispering.
'In truth, I don't know,' he replied, 'but it wouldn't surprise me.'
'Why? What do you know?'
'I *know* nothing. But there's something about Tim Byrne. If I could

be dangerously honest here, I wouldn't trust him with my cat.'
I wondered how many other people thought that way. Was I the only one who found him charismatic? Everybody else I had seen around him was as charmed by him as I had been, so what were we missing?
'But everybody loves him,' I protested, as much to myself as to Pete.
He laughed, 'Maybe it's a gay thing.'
I joined in, 'So you don't fancy him, then?'
He overacted a great shudder then, with an added 'ugh' face, 'Not if he were the only man left and I was drunk.'
I was a little stunned. Wow, had I got this wrong. I should have made sure I introduced him to Beth – she would have seen through him from the start.

We parted with a 'leave it with me' from him, and he promised to keep me up to date once he knew how it was going to play out. We walked out through the garden together as he made his way to his car, and I was going home, feeling more at ease than I had in days: I had had a great day at work, and now I had off-loaded my story into the most sympathetic of ears. As I reached the lych-gate that separated the garden from the road something pink caught my eye, and I turned to see Alice sitting alone at one of the outside tables. There were books and papers in front of her, but she wasn't working on them – she was looking straight at me. We were a long trek from her school. Was she here to keep an eye on me? Had she been watching me with Pete? Was she spying for Tim?
Oh, great, Kelly, let's add paranoia to your list of mental imbalances.
I realised my heart was pounding a bit as I said a casual 'hello'.
Then, 'I've not seen you here before,' with a smile.
'Oh, I can just work in peace here,' she said, her expression revealing nothing. 'Your local, is it?'
That was not an idle question. She was fishing.
'Close enough,' I said, as casually as I could manage, and left before she drew me in to more conversation than I was comfortable with.

On the short walk home I examined my own motives: why was I wary of her?

As soon as I got home I updated Beth by phone. Just because she was geographically distant for now didn't mean I wasn't going to keep her in the loop. That was another lesson I had learned in all this. It's often the talking about things that gives us the perspective we need, and Beth was only ever going to talk sense and sympathy. I put the radio on then, had a long and lovely bath, and got into my comfiest pyjamas. While I knew it wasn't all going to go away in an instant, I was beginning to feel more relaxed. I suppose that meant I had dropped my guard, though I'm not sure I could have prevented what happened next however alert I had been.

When I had been on the sofa with a book for about half an hour, and was beginning to think about making it an early night, I heard the most chilling sound of all – the key in the door. I couldn't think what he was doing here; surely I had made myself clear last time. Not knowing whether he came in peace or fury, in a moment of clarity and self-preservation I grabbed my phone from the coffee table in front of me, pressed record, and put it out of sight under the sofa, just as he came at me with a terrifying sneer on his face.
'Been talking to our new friend, have we?'
I was in no doubt what he was referring to.
'I don't know what you mean,' I protested feebly.
'Pete Compton rang me 'for comment',' he snarled. 'Seems we have a little difference of opinion.'
I said nothing, just felt myself freeze as he began the awful ritual again – he was undressing, just enough, as he spoke. I knew what was coming.
'Thinks she was raped, does she?'
'I never used that word,' I was still hoping this would all go away.
'Pete did, and he didn't pluck it out of the air. So that's what you think, is it?'
He didn't wait for me to answer.

'That wasn't rape, trust me. I'll show you what rape is.'
And before I could think, his hand was across my face again, more vicious, more startling than the last time, and he followed it with a punch into my stomach, leaving me bent over and gasping for breath.
'Come on, then – fight!' and he hit me again, in the side of the head this time. 'If I'm raping you, you'd fight, so fight!'
I think I whimpered something incoherent, but I certainly didn't fight back. I knew instinctively that would wind him up, be all the worse for me.
He pushed me to the floor and was on top of me before I could even put up so much a hand to stop him, but, as he pushed himself inside me, I had a brief lucid moment, just enough to make sure there would be evidence, no question about consent.
'I don't want this, Tim,' I said clearly, making sure I was angled towards where the phone was.
'We've been over that – you always want it. Now just shut up,' and he punctuated his instruction with a thrust so sudden and so deep inside me that it was way beyond discomfort. I think I must have yelled then, as I was slapped again.
'Are you listening to me?'
I tried to do as I was told, in the hope it would be over more quickly that way, but I know I said other things, without form or thought, pleading, asking him to stop, willing it to be done. As he accelerated towards whatever was his climax I was in more and more pain: when he threw me down he had taken no care, of course, and my head was bent at a strange angle against the front of the sofa. With each brutal thrust I was being jammed tighter and tighter against it, until I was struggling to breathe and truly thought my neck was going to break. Then, just as I was hoping this would soon be at an end, the sofa jerked backwards under the pressure, and I could see the edge of my phone. If he saw it, realised what it was doing there, any defence I had would be over. Both in desperation for him not to spot it and the genuine pain of my position, I screamed then, long and loud. I knew it was a risk – who knew what fresh violence it would bring –

but instead of provoking more obvious brutality, sickeningly, he seemed to be enjoying this evidence of my pain and discomfort, and, surprisingly gently, put one hand over my mouth and held my nose. For the first time, hearing his 'gentle' 'shh' like an echo of sweeter moments, I was genuinely frightened I might die. As I began to see spots I noticed the look on his face I had seen in more tender moments, the one that says he's nearly finished, and as I heard the usual grunt, he let go of my face and I gulped in air. In completion, he pushed himself so far inside me it was as if he was trying to climb in, and held himself there. It was agonising. There was no doubt he was turned on by his power over me, and I was overwhelmed by loathing for him at that moment.

After what seemed an age of this grunting, sweating pig pinning me down with his full spent body-weight, he stood up, leading with the ever-present smile, though I saw it as a leer now.
'So,' he said as he pulled himself together, 'are we clear now?'
'About what?' I muttered.
'If you speak to Pete Compton, or anybody else about this, they won't believe you, you know.'
'I know.'
'Good. Your word, the word of a deranged groupie, against the local celebrity, the new mayor, who couldn't possibly risk losing what he has just won, by sexual impropriety.'
His arrogance was breath-taking.
'I know,' I said again, already weeping.
Finally, he moved towards the door.
'Oh, and don't be thinking about doing a Monica Lewinsky. My DNA is all over this place, so who would care about one more spot?'
I knew he was right. I just wanted him to leave before he saw the phone, so I shifted my body to make sure I was between it and him. He pulled my key out of his pocket, then.
'Thank you,' I said.
'For what? Oh, you thought I was going to give this back to you?'
And he laughed, then tossed it in his hand a couple of times and slipped it back into his pocket. He was just taunting me, using the

key and its symbolism to demonstrate his power again.
What had I ever seen in him? Why hadn't I spotted this vile bully under the practised veneer?

I was right back at square one now. Having thought I was beginning to see daylight - sharing it with Beth and taking her advice, having a really good day at work, speaking at length to Pete Compton - I was bereft again. I would very much have preferred to feel numb, but not only was the physical pain coming at me from all directions – my neck, my face, my foot, my insides –the humiliation was overriding all of it. I managed to hold myself together just long enough to hear the front door close, and, assuming he had now actually left, I howled like a small child.

Incongruously, I slept then, right where I was on the front room floor, amongst the rags of my now-tattered pyjamas and displaced furniture. I woke, shivering and sore, after a couple of hours, and my first thought (at last – a clear one!) was for my phone. I reached under the sofa and found it quickly, only to find a dead black screen staring back at me. Of course, the battery had run out, but how long ago? How much of the ordeal had it caught before it died? I got up then, slowly and carefully, and grabbed the charger and plugged it in. I knew it wouldn't come on immediately, but I didn't want to leave it, I wanted to be there the very second it came to life.

While I waited I broke all the rules. Oh, I know what we're all told to do in these situations, but equally I knew he would have an answer for them all, so what was the point of preserving the evidence? First, I took off what was left of my night-clothes and threw them into the kitchen bin - he could claim them as evidence that I liked it rough and saw my cheap Tesco polyester as disposable; then I went into the bathroom and had a thorough wash – his DNA all over me (and inside me) would prove only that we had had sex, which we had done so often before that it was no evidence at all; besides, I really needed to soothe myself, and warm water seemed the gentlest option. It was then I realised why he had kept my key: more than just the power of knowing he could come back any time he liked, it was evidence that I had invited him in, welcomed his attentions, if he ever needed to prove it. I was so glad I had arranged for Cliff to come and change the lock.

7.

My phone had recorded the whole event, and in startling clarity. Of course, taken as it was from under the sofa, there were no visuals, but it still made for very uncomfortable listening. I didn't even listen to all of it, just the beginning to check it had in fact recorded, then ran to the end to make sure it was all there. I was a long way from being ready to hear it yet. My dilemma now, though, was what to do with it. Yes, I know I should have gone straight to the police, but still the embarrassment overrode every other reaction. If I played it to them, to strangers, what would they make of it? And what would they do with it? I couldn't guarantee it wouldn't be passed around the local station, whether as titillation for leering men, or in the spirit of gossip about a local dignitary. I knew that, before I could expose myself to those possibilities, I needed to be a great deal stronger than I felt right now. Should I tell Beth? Yes, of course I should, but I still didn't know if I was going to – she would hear my weakness, the whimpering and pleading, be witness to the worst moments of my life, and she would never again be able to see me as just her friend. I felt as if our relationship would always be tainted by my very vulnerability, somehow. So, should I turn to Pete again? Absolutely not! He had obviously betrayed me, told Tim about my earlier accusations. It was Pete who had put me in danger in the first place, and I wasn't going to risk him abusing my trust again. And I was more sad than angry about that – I thought I had found a new friend. So I held onto it, kept it to myself, hoping, I suppose, that some sort of destination for it would emerge when the time was right, when I could face the dreadful (and I had no doubt it would be dreadful) fallout.

In the meantime, Cliff came as planned, and changed my front door lock. While he was there he added locks to my windows, and even though my flat was on the first floor, it gave me some comfort. He asked no awkward questions, just chatted inconsequentially while he was working, and left me my new set of keys. It was just after he left that I had a phone call from Pete, wanting to update me on his conversation with Tim Byrne, I assumed. As soon as I saw his name on the screen I clicked it over to voice – I wasn't ready to speak to him just yet - then listened to the message he left. It was bland and non-committal,
'Hi, Kelly, Pete here. Just thought I'd bring you up to date.'
Shouldn't that be the other way round? Shouldn't I be the one doing the updating? He really had no idea what his indiscretion had led to.
'Give me a call when you get the chance.'
Probably not, Pete.

For the next few days I just kept going, still rebuilding relationships at work, trying to separate what had happened from the life I was trying to lead. It was really difficult: every time I thought I had successfully pushed it back into a dark recess somewhere in my mind where it wouldn't surface till I was ready to deal with it, something trivial would remind me, and it all came back. Snippets of unrequited love songs, anything on the news about politics or elections, even fish and chips. Tim hadn't tried to make contact in any way, and I cancelled my weekly order for the local paper, knowing if I did read it I would see both his name and Pete's. I was determined not to allow being in my flat alone to become a big issue, and I had to make a conscious effort to 'reclaim the space' for myself. I tried a bit of reconditioning, touched things to remind myself they were mine, stood on the ghastly spot by the sofa and deliberately conjured up mental pictures of happier moments there – Beth and a bottle of wine, dinner with Geoff – and finally decided to resort to a bit of redecorating. After work on the Friday, about ten days after he had attacked me in my own home, I went to a DIY store and bought huge buckets of magnolia paint, a roller and tray, then dragged Beth round to give me a hand early the next morning. I didn't tell her why, though. We set to with a will, and it took us only the weekend to transform the front room into the blandest room on the planet, all soft neutral tones – just what I needed. I threw away the round purple patterned cushions and bought new ones, square with stripey autumn colours, as far from the old ones as I could find, and found a giant throw to disguise the sofa. Beth is too astute, though, and did challenge me, just a little.

'Why are you covering up your lovely pearl-grey walls? There's nothing wrong with them.'

'I need a change,' was all I could come up with.

She knew what I was trying to do, just not exactly why, and didn't ask again. She contributed a new set of mugs, and I was happy to get rid of the rest of the original set, and not just because there was one missing now.

Through all of this Pete rang again and again (in truth it was only once a day), leaving increasingly worried-sounding messages. Finally, more than a week after the attack, sitting in my shiny new room, I decided I could face the inevitable conversation, and answered his call.

'Kelly, I've been really worried. Did you get my messages?'

'Yes,' I said as neutrally as I could, 'I got them, all of them.'

Well, maybe not so neutral.

'Why didn't you call me back? I wanted to let you know what happened with Tim Byrne.'

Oh, I knew only too well what had happened with Tim Byrne, but I wasn't about to share it with the town's mouthpiece.

'He denied it all, of course.'

'I'm sure he did.'

'I suppose we should talk about what we do next.'

I cut him off.

'There's nothing to talk about. He's denied it, you can't print it, it's over.'

I was ready to hang up then, but he stopped me, sensing, I suppose, that all was not well between us.

'Kelly, what's wrong? We need to do something about this man.'

I laughed then.

'I think you've done enough.'

'What do you mean?' and I could hear the wariness in his voice.

'You told him what I said.'

He denied it.

'I didn't, Kelly. I said nothing. I didn't identify you.'

'Then why did he come round here, furious with me?'

There was a pause from the other end. Then,

'I'm so sorry, Kelly. I was careful not to name you. I'm better than that.'

'I'm sure you think you are.'

'Oh, don't be like that. Please.'

That was his fatal error.

'Like what? I confided in you, told you about Tim, and what happened? I'm the one in trouble. I'm the one he takes it out on. You made me unsafe in my own home.' I was shouting now.

'That's not how it happened...'

'Oh, where you there? Was it you he came to see?'

'Kelly, please. I promise you, I told him nothing. He must have worked out where my info came from. I'm so sorry.'

I suppose I should have been relieved that Tim knew it was me – that would mean he didn't have a string of eager victims.

'Not half as sorry as I am,' still almost shouting. 'It's over. He's got what he wanted. Please don't call me again.'

'But Kelly,' he tried again, 'we have to stop him.'

'You stop him, any way you like, but leave me out of it. I don't trust you.'

'That's not fair...'

But again I cut him off.

'Fair to whom? I'm done, Pete. Don't call me again.'

And I hung up, actually feeling a bit smug. I had said the things I wanted to say, had closed that little chapter. I wouldn't be so naïve in future.

Over the next few months I could have persuaded myself that it had all gone away, that I had filed it in the archive section of my memory banks. Work was actually a joy: we won a couple of huge and ongoing orders from a PR firm and their clients, which meant we were busier than ever; we expanded our working space until we were considering buying much larger premises (and managing the move would probably fall to me, hurrah); we had taken on two newbies in the office to help manage all the admin; the technical and creative teams were growing exponentially. It was lovely to see all our hard work paying off, and I had always been at my best as part of a dynamic and success-focussed team. The ubiquitous 'after-work drink' was a weekly date, and we even popped over the road for a team lunch, on the company, from time to time.

Beth continued to be my rock. Whenever she was at home, which was most weekends at least, we would be found cooking for each other, going to our favourite haunts or making plans to do so. She had even persuaded me to complete a couple of online courses with her, so I could now boast a diploma in Keeping Succulents and Cacti and another in Colour for Wellbeing, of all things! I also saw more of my family than I had in years, to my parents' delight, visiting them on some weekends when Beth wasn't available. I took no interest at all in local politics, and very little in anything wider, and allowed my Guardians membership to lapse without a second thought. Pete had left me a couple of voice messages asking to meet me, but I ignored them until they stopped. I had become quite dull again, which felt like full circle.

It was a chance meeting with Geoff, of all people, that first gave me pause in what I had thought was a healthy trajectory of recovery. I was indulging in a little idle shopping (more a bit of a stroll round the town centre, punctuated by coffee and cake breaks, to be honest) one Saturday when Beth was working away, when I heard my name as I passed tables outside Café Nero. I turned to see Geoff sitting with a gorgeous creature, a glossy blonde vision in mauve and cream, both of them with radiating smiles. As I walked towards them, Geoff stood to greet me, and the welcome on his face was genuine – he was truly pleased to see me.

'Kelly, how lovely to see you,' he said as he stood to greet me.

He kissed me warmly on both cheeks, then turned to his companion.

'You haven't met Ali,' he said, and his smile told me all I needed to know about their relationship – this was a little cocoon of mutual adoration.

'Ali – this is Kelly, *the* Kelly.'

Ali stood up beside him, and actually hugged me. I don't remember the last time I was hugged by a stranger.

'How lovely to meet you at last,' she said, and I could tell she meant it. 'I've heard so much about you. Please, will you stay and have a coffee with us?'

I didn't have to think about that – these two radiated welcome. And it wasn't like I was busy doing anything else.

'What can I get you?' asked Geoff, heading for the door of the café, but Ali pulled him back gently,

'No, I'll get it. You two have catching up to do. Chocolate, isn't it, Kelly?'

And they laughed together, as I realised Geoff must have told her about my go-to comfort drink.

'No, just a tea, thanks,' I said as I sat.

Geoff pulled my hand into his and looked me squarely in the eyes.

'I can't tell you how pleased I am to catch up with you,' he said. 'I've missed you.'

I paused before I answered him, to make sure I was speaking from the heart.

'Do you know, I've missed you, too.' I said, realising as I said it that it was true. Geoff had been a steadying influence on me. For all that our relationship had, in some ways, bored itself to death, it represented security, a life untroubled by the drama that had characterised my life since him. If I hadn't sent him away I would never have met the predator Tim Byrne, or the treacherous Pete Compton, and I would have been safe. If I had stayed with him, my life would most likely be a much duller existence, and I think I would have been thankful for that in hindsight.

We then spent an easy half an hour in the sun, the three of us, all chatting like we had been friends for ever. Ali already knew the stories, our shared background, and was clearly a grown-up – no childish jealousy of me and my place in his history. In fact, at one point, she thanked me for making him an adult, and gave me the credit for turning him into the man she now loved. For his part, Geoff had clearly taken the lessons from my untimely dismissal of him – he deferred to Ali, included her, asked her opinion, treated her as an equal, all the things I thought had been missing when we were together. But I couldn't be certain I had anything to do with the transformation, if, indeed, that is what it was: maybe he had always been like this and I just didn't notice. I was aware now, thanks to Tim, that my judgement was not all it should have been, so maybe this was the real Geoff after all. Whatever, this was a very happy little union, and I basked in their warmth and inclusion.

It was a simple question from Ali that threw me.
'So, Kelly, are you seeing anyone?'
The direct and truthful answer was easy,
'No, not at the moment,' but suddenly inside my head questions were competing for consideration: why wasn't I seeing anybody? Why had there been nobody (nobody real, that is) since Geoff? Was I deliberately keeping people (men) at a distance? Did I want to be with anybody?
For good measure I added the well-worn,
'Happy on my own for now,' though I had no idea if that was actually the truth. I wasn't happy at all, but, worryingly if I had allowed myself to think in such terms, I wasn't unhappy either. I was neutral, nothing, not feeling anything. It was going to take a bit of thinking about.
We parted with kisses and promises to get together again soon, and I thought we probably would: they had been refreshing

company and were obviously devoted to each other. Well done, Geoff – no less than you deserve after the shabby way I treated you.

I chose to walk home from the town centre: a couple of miles of exercise would give me space to reflect on what had just popped up in my head like a meerkat from a burrow. In concentrating on my recovery, my present condition, I had not given a thought to my future, at least not beyond work, in a long time. There had been no searching for another project to fill my time, no light-hearted (or even serious) discussions with Beth about where I saw myself in five years' time, and not a single hint of a relationship, not even a date. I was living in the present only, and I wasn't sure how healthy that was for me. What would this emotional numbness do to my sanity in the long term? Did it mean I was suppressing those dreadful events after the election, in favour of a spurious and fragile peace?

Of course it did. Time to wake up, Kelly. I resolved on the spot to pull myself together, and to do that I knew I had to start facing up to the things in my past that I had allowed to limit my present. If I left those barriers in place, then Tim Byrne would still be exerting a form of control over me, however remotely, and I couldn't let that happen.

As soon as I got home I pulled out my phone and flicked to the recording. I sat and looked at the screen for a while, trying to find the strength to face it all again. I knew I should probably have called Beth, waited until she was with me for support, but I hadn't shared it with her in the first place, and it would be all the more shocking to her for that. Besides, this was my journey; I was the only one who could assume responsibility for myself and my future, not to mention the fact that I had made the (in retrospect ludicrous) decision to manage it alone; so that's what I would do now.

It was awful listening. Not having heard it in full before, I had allowed myself to forget how distressing it was. I was frightened and in pain all over again, and my hands were shaking before I was even halfway through. At the end, I sat and sobbed quietly for some minutes, until I realised I was rocking like a bear in a cage. What had I started? Now I felt worse than I had before I heard it through. But surely that was a more truthful response than trying to pretend it hadn't happened at all? Surely I needed to face up to it, confront it, suck it up if you like, so I could actually process it properly? I resolved to listen to it again, now. I knew it would still be painful, but maybe I was trying to desensitise myself. I waited long enough to make myself a strong coffee, then listened to it all a second time. By the end I was still shaking, but I wasn't rocking any more, so maybe the desensitisation programme was working already.

The next step was to decide what to do with it, if anything. I went through all the options I had considered before – the police, the newspapers, maybe even confronting Tim with it directly (not a chance!) – and came up with nothing useful. Maybe I should just delete it, discard it, as a sort of symbolic shedding of the past. But I knew I wasn't going to do that. There was a tiny voice in the back of my mind that was saying 'evidence'. Maybe time would reveal a way of using it to my advantage. Oh, I don't mean revenge, but perhaps one day someone might need to see Tim's true colours, and this little shard of dynamite on my phone would give them what they needed.

The answer presented itself a week or two later, when, just after lunch one Tuesday, Pete Compton walked into my office with Dorrett. She had mentioned to us all that the local paper wanted to do a piece about us. It seems they had been running a series of articles about successful local companies (as I no longer read the Chronicle I hadn't seen it) and somebody had suggested us. We certainly fitted into their bracket – we were busy, profitable and respected, and the expansion was solid evidence of all that. They would be speaking mostly to Dorrett, as the whole business was her brainchild, her baby, and she remained the driving force behind our enthusiasm and commitment. In fact, we already knew their strongest angle that we were mostly women, or, as Dorrett called us, 'sisters doing it for themselves'. We acknowledged it was one of our strengths, and were happy to demonstrate the levels of cooperation and competence we were so proud of. But they wanted more than one voice, and needed someone to do the gruntwork – showing them around the premises, talking them through the processes and so on, and, as admin team leader I was the one Dorrett had asked to lead that aspect of the visit. I had barely given Pete Compton a second thought since I had felt so betrayed by his indiscretion all that time ago, so I was a little taken aback when he appeared in the doorway of my office with Dorrett.

'Kelly, this is Pete Compton from the Chronicle. He's here for the tour.'

Before I could say anything he approached my desk, hand outstretched and a warm smile on his face.

'We've met,' he said, and took my hand. 'Lovely to see you again.'

'Then I'll leave you to it,' said Dorrett as she backed out of the room.

'Of course it had to be you,' I said archly, almost before she had closed the door. 'I suppose you had better sit down.'

But he didn't sit, just stood in front of my desk, head on one side, looking at me with an uncomfortable intensity.

'I've thought about you a lot, Kelly,' he said then, and I could detect no edge.

'That's odd,' I said, not dropping my own hostility for a second, 'you've barely crossed my mind.'

'Ok,' he said, and this time there was a clear decisiveness, 'if we're going to work together we have to clear the air first.'

'There's nothing to clear.' I was doing it again – I was already so invested in my position that I felt I couldn't drop it. How quickly I became that someone I didn't like.

'That's not how I see it,' he said as he finally sat. 'You're angry with me because you thought I had betrayed you. Well, there is another side to the story, and I'd like you to listen to it.'

I wanted to refuse to listen to his story, but realised at the same time that it may well prick the little bubble I had built around myself. In the light of my recent self-revelations, that would probably be a good thing, if only to face up to another little slice of my history. When he then indicated for me to sit, too, I complied meekly under his assertiveness.

'Thank you,' he said, and launched into what I realised quickly was a well-rehearsed tale – he had thought long and hard about what he was going to say to me if he ever got the chance, and now was his one chance. I didn't interrupt him.

'I did talk to Tim Byrne after you told me what had happened on the election night, but not only did I not mention your name, I didn't even give him any details about what you told me. I know how to do my job, Kelly, and I would never put anybody at risk for a story.'

I wanted to believe him.

'I asked him if he had any skeletons, that's all. His answer was arrogant beyond belief, especially considering what I knew about him. He said, and I quote, 'when you're in the public eye you can't afford skeletons.' I pushed him, just a little: 'So no hidden bank accounts or illegitimate children then? Am I going to find you have a criminal record?' That was when he laughed, and I knew he was laughing at me, not with me: he was daring me to try and find the dirt. He's a nasty piece of work, Kelly.'

'Then how come he was on my doorstep the same day?'

'He may be vile, but he's not stupid. The last thing I said to him was, 'Not even a bit of sexual impropriety? If you have any secret girlfriends let me know and I'll go and have a chat with them.' And that is as close as I came to mentioning you at all.'

I knew his version was closer to the truth than Tim's would ever be. Tim believed only his own truth.

'He told me you wouldn't believe me.'

I was very quiet now, just looking down, staring at my hands in my lap.

'Well, I told you I did, and I stand by that.'

I had been wrong again, so wrong. I sat for a moment, to try and digest all this. I wasn't sure how much more self-revelation I could take in such a short space of time.

'I'm sorry,' I was almost whispering. 'I was wrong about you, wasn't I?'

'Yes,' he said without accusation, 'but more importantly, what do we do about it?'

I couldn't think then. I needed to get some distance from it all first, take my usual time to reflect, before deciding on any course of action.

'Let me think,' I said, and I didn't care if that sounded feeble. 'But not now.'

'Ok,' he agreed readily, clearly happy to have opened a pathway to resolution between us. 'Shall we get the work out of the way first, and we can think about this later?'

I was already much better at compartmentalising than I had been in the past, so our tour of the offices and workrooms was almost pleasant, and I found myself warming to him all over again as the day went on. As it turned out, between chatting to almost everybody there, asking astute questions, and a long interview with Dorrett, he was with us for the rest of the day. Just before 5 o'clock Jenna moved into her informal social secretary role, and, with Dorrett's blessing, invited Pete to join us in the pub. He was pleased to have been asked, and turned out to be very good company in a group. They were all at ease with him, and we knew our company's story was safe with him – this would be good coverage. More to the point, I realised I could trust him after all, and I knew what I was going to do with my phone recording.

He was the first to leave the pub and handed his 'confetti' to each of us before he went 'in case there's anything you'd like to add'. I had long ago discarded the original one he had given me, so I took a new one, knowing I was likely to use it soon.

Before I committed myself to that course, however, I made the decision to come clean with Beth, and, let's face it, not before time!

I took my time, getting home and having dinner, then clearing up and settling down with a large glass in my hand before I picked up the phone. She was somewhere in Norfolk this week, and I knew her schedule. I waited till I knew she would be finished with work for the day, and dialled her hotel number. She answered with her usual cheery 'Beth' and I took a deep breath.

'I have something to tell you. But first I should say I know I should have told you ages ago.'

It was really hard to make myself say the words. This was going to be harder than I thought.

'Go on,' she prompted. 'I'm listening.'

I found myself going round the houses till I could force myself to say it.

'You remember when I made you come over and redecorate my lounge?'

'Hardly 'made me'. I was a volunteer.'

'Ok, ok. Well, I needed to clear that space out.'

'I know.'

'But you don't know why.'

I kept pausing. This was ridiculous. This was Beth, for goodness' sake. She wasn't going to judge me, and I realised I was judging myself again. Finally, I plunged in.

'Tim attacked me. He raped me in my own home.'

I had never said the word before, and if I had been hoping for a great rush of relief that I had finally said it now, I was disappointed. I felt only the anxiety of having excluded my friend from the most cataclysmic event of my life.

Now it was her turn to pause, and I heard her exhale.

'And you've held on to this news for all this time?'

'I'm sorry, Beth. I didn't know how to say it.'

'And you're doing it over the phone, when there's nothing I can do? I can't even give you the slap around the head you deserve! Why on earth didn't you say anything till now?'

'It was too hard to tell anybody. And I didn't want you to see me as the poor little victim. You'd never have been able to see me in the quite the same way again.'

'How could you think that?' she said, and I could hear her exasperation.

'There's more,' I said before she could threaten me further. 'I have it on my phone.'

'What do you mean you have it on your phone?'

'I recorded it.'

I heard her gasp.

Surprisingly, we didn't talk for long after that. Beth was all for ditching work for the rest of the week and heading back down the motorway to be with me. I managed to reassure her – I had been living with this for so long now another couple of days before she could hug me wouldn't make much difference. She asked me what I was going to do with the recording, and I answered truthfully that I didn't know yet (though I did know I wouldn't be playing it to her – it was too distressing for friends' ears); she tried to tease out some details from me, but she was a bit half-hearted about it – we both knew we'd rather do that face-to-face, didn't want the distance to reinforce the barriers I had put up by excluding her again, so we promised to spend time together over the weekend, and maybe draft the next plan of action; she reassured me that she still loved me, and thought no less of me for not telling her sooner (with an added side of comedy threat). When we said our goodbyes I knew I had done the right thing. Yes, I should probably have done it sooner, but I had done it now. I was even looking forward to the weekend, to shedding the biggest of the obstacles to my sanity and wellbeing – rediscovering an honest relationship with Beth.

My lighter mood worked well until the weekend. It was then that all the wheels fell off in spectacular fashion.

8.

I phoned Pete the same evening, just after I had spoken to Beth. The call started casually enough, me repeating my apologies for misjudging him, a little about today's visit and the ensuing article ('you're going to like it'), and then I got down to the real reason for my call.
'Actually, Pete, I have something for you.'
'Ooh, I'm intrigued. Tell me, is it about Tim Byrne?'
'How did you guess?' I trilled a little nervously.
'Wonderful. I've dedicated my life to bringing him down, you know.'
He was speaking light-heartedly, but I suspected there was more than a little truth in the words.
'What have you got? Ooh, please tell me you've got art.'
'Probably better than art,' I said. I knew I was teasing him, but it wasn't deliberate – I wanted him to know that what I had was substantial, but I certainly wasn't going to discuss it over the phone.
'Can you meet me tomorrow after work?'
'I most certainly can.' I could hear his excitement.
'And the boyfriend won't mind losing you for the evening?' my turn to keep it light.
'Oh, he's gone now. I'm free as a bird. Can do as I like.'
He didn't sound at all bothered.
'How about a repeat of our last date? Say 6 o'clock at the Beggar's?'
'Perfect. See you then.'

I went straight to the Beggar's Arms after work and took a pint into the garden while I waited for Pete. He wasn't late, and I saw him coming across the garden with a pint for himself and a menu under his arm. He put them down on the table then came and sat beside me on the wooden bench.

'I'm glad you called,' he said, and I could tell he meant it, though I wasn't sure if it was more about being pleased to see me than getting some evidence to achieve his mission. 'Shall we order before we talk?'

I had installed the menu app a long time ago, and we ordered sandwiches and soup from our phones. After today's visit to Bellows, we had a lot to chat about until the food came and we wouldn't be disturbed again, and I kept it bland with a couple of innocent little stories about my colleagues, while he reassured me he had liked what he'd seen and would be reviewing us very favourably. Finally, I took a breath and began my torrid tale. My call with Beth the previous evening had served as a rehearsal somehow, so this time the key words came slightly more easily,

'Tim Byrne raped me,' and I took a big bite of my sandwich while I waited for Pete's reaction. There wasn't one at first, at all. In fact, it was rather comical, as he froze, sandwich in hand, mouth open, and just stared at me.

I joined in with the comedy routine and tapped his chin upwards to close his mouth, with,

'Not your most appealing look.'

Finally, he regained some composure.

'Do you mean the night you told me about before? Election night?'

'No, that was just as I told you. It was unpleasant enough, sure, but he came back after I told you about it. He thought he'd show me the difference between that night and 'real rape', apparently.'

'Shit, Kelly,' he exclaimed. 'I had no idea.'

'How could you? I didn't tell anybody. I couldn't. Once I'd told you, and you tried to get some confirmation from him, he came back. I thought he was going to kill me at one point.'

'No wonder you didn't trust me.'

'I felt silenced, to be honest.'

'I'm not surprised.'

To his credit, Pete's first concern was for me.

'And are you OK now?'

I thought before I answered that.

'I think so,' I ventured. Well, I will be. At least, I'm beginning to get there.'

'Can you tell me what happened?'

'I can, and I can actually do better than that. But first we need to be clear about what happens after I tell you. I'm going to need confidentiality, big-time. He frightened me. Still does.'

'Fair enough,' he said, trying not to slop his pint in his excitement. 'OK, here's how it works: I won't know exactly what to do until I know what I've got - we don't print anything controversial without double confirmation, proper evidence, so we can't be challenged. Also, we're a small set-up, and can't afford to be sued, so we have to run everything that could possibly be libellous through our lawyers, so there will certainly be protection from them.'

I was nodding along. So far so good.

'They make sure we avoid any chance of it. Win or lose, lawyers are expensive, and if we actually lost we'd go under.'

He continued, warming to his argument, through mouthfuls of sandwich and beer.

'At some point, if we do this right, he's going to know about it, but not before it's all sewn up, and too public for him to be able to fight back. With any luck, he'll know nothing until the police are banging on his door with the handcuffs! We will not name you, ever, without your full cooperation, but that's a long way down the line.'

I didn't know if I would ever be ready for that, and said so.

'Then you'll be witness A,' and we laughed together. I was imagining the court artist's impression of me already.

'So, do you think you can trust me with whatever it is you have?'

'I guess so,' I said, and he sat back while I gave him an outline of the attack. I didn't give him the tiny details - I didn't tell him about the sofa moving, the tossing of the key, the indescribable pain – no one needed to know any of that, and I was already in tears just telling it, without adding to the embarrassment by letting him feel my vulnerability. By the time I had finished he was looking

quite shaken. I wondered briefly how he was going to look when I told him about the phone, and chastised myself inwardly for anticipating the drama. When I finished by telling him about changing the locks and redecorating, he nodded.
'This man is contemptible,' he said, and it sounded like a considered evaluation rather than a snap judgement or insult. 'I have to get him now. I want to bring him down.'
'Well, I can help there,' I said, already beginning to recover my composure. 'I recorded the whole thing.'
Pete was as stunned as I had hoped he would be.
'You did what? How?'
'On my phone. I've got it all. Oh, no pictures, no actual footage, but you can hear all of it, from start to finish.'
'How on earth…?' he began.
'I guess I thought faster than him for the only time in my life. I turned it on when I heard him coming in.'
He was really animated now.
'Kelly, that's amazing! We've got him! With that kind of evidence he couldn't deny it!'
'But you can't make it public. Remember, you promised.'
'I know, and I won't. But I will find a way to make it work for us. Can I listen to it?'
I think he worried for a moment that it wasn't real, that the 'recording' was in my imagination. I reassured him.
'You can hear it, but not while I'm here. I can't listen to it with anybody else. It's too painful. I haven't even shared it with my best friend.'
Bless Beth – she hadn't even asked to hear it. 'Promise me you'll listen to it only when you're alone.'
'I promise.' He was eager to get his hands on the means to finish off Tim.
'And you won't share it with anyone else.'
'I promise.'
'And you'll let me know before you decide what to do with it?'
'I promise! Can you send it to me?'
'I think the safest way is WhatsApp. What do you think?'

'Yes,' he agreed, 'end-to-end encryption.'
'You sound like an advert for secret squirrel now,' I laughed, then paused before pressing the right buttons on my phone.

It was some time later that I found out this meeting had been not quite as private as I hoped - Alice was in the garden again.

I found it difficult to settle for the rest of the evening: not only was the worst moment of my life out there, being scrutinised by a virtual stranger, but I had lost some of my control over it. I felt vulnerable again, but had to take some comfort from my renewed trust in Pete's integrity. Before I went to bed I rang Beth again, ostensibly to say goodnight, but in reality I wanted to share my anxiety. I needed to tell somebody (and there was no one else I could share it with) that I had given the recording to Pete, not only to keep her up to date, but also to hear her reassurances, which, of course, she gave willingly. A tiny piece of me still struggled to trust what Pete would do with it. He was a journalist, after all, whose instinct would be to seek to create the biggest impact from my footage, and therefore could be playing fast and loose with my security.
'You've done the right thing. Trust your judgement,' Beth said, but that was the problem: I still didn't know if my judgement was worth anything!

The following evening, the Thursday, I had a brief phone call from Pete. I answered nervously, but he was keen to put me at my ease straight away with an immediate 'don't worry – you're still totally anonymous.'
He sounded very excited, though.
'I can't stop cos we're just going to press, but we've started, Kelly. We're on our way. I'm going to bring him down, just you watch.'
I asked him for detail, but he was like a little boy with a big secret, and just told me to look out for the front page on Friday.

I managed to get some sleep, and went into work on the Friday looking forward to seeing the article Pete had written about us, not to mention whatever it was on the front page. I was not alone: when I arrived there was a copy of the Chronicle on each desk and workstation, and a beaming Dorrett was in the middle of the office handing out croissants and freshly-brewed coffee. The Bellows article was long, over two whole pages in the middle of the paper. There were photographs - the building and workshop, a selection of some of our best merchandise, and a whole-staff photo, all of us smiling and waving at the camera. This article was more than a biography, it was like free advertising – Pete had loved us! All the things we hoped to see were in there – our philosophy of transparency and self-development, our commitment to product quality and client confidence, and lots of individual comments from colleagues, all saying what a wonderful place it was to work. Little real work was done for the rest of the day – we were all too buzzing with pride.

More importantly for me, however, was the front page Pete had referred to. At the bottom left-hand corner was a photo of Tim Byrne, under a small banner that said 'Our Mayor – too good to be true? See Editorial p.2'
I turned to page 2, almost surreptitiously. I don't know why I felt compelled to keep it to myself, and they could all have seen it if they wanted to, but I knew this was what Pete had told me about, and I needed to make sure I was not identified. Besides, I was genuinely curious to see how he had handled it. The article was only about a third of a column, and was part editorial, part fishing. It was skilfully written and avoided naming anybody, even Tim – the picture on the front page was the only reference to him. The paper obviously took seriously their roles as the politicians' conscience and readers' champion, and the thrust of the piece was 'the Guardians are ambitious, so we need to make sure they are fit for office before they become really big', and hinted that there might be things we needed to know. It ended by asking anybody with information or evidence to get in touch with them. Bravo, Pete, though I wondered how they had got it past the lawyers – it was bit close to the bone. I sent him a quick text saying pretty

much that and tucked the paper in my bag to read at my leisure later. I also sent Beth a similar text, letting her know that Pete had been true to his word, and inviting her over when she got back from Norfolk so we could look at it together. I got a reply from her just as I was leaving the office at the end of the day, and was delighted to see she had already left Norfolk and was suggesting we meet at the Beggar's for dinner and a pore through the paper.

I didn't bother going home, just went straight to the Beggar's Arms – it was a pleasant place to wait, and Beth wasn't going to be long. As I entered through the garden, I was a little surprised to find Alice sitting at a table, facing the gateway as if she were waiting for somebody. It would have been rude, not to mention obvious, if I ignored her; after all, I had to walk right past her to get into the bar for my drink, and she didn't know I was wary of her. I was quite taken aback when she stood up to greet me as if I were the one she had been waiting for.
'Hi, Kelly.'
I couldn't read anything into her simple greeting, and, not for the first time, wondered if it was just my paranoia that was causing my suspicion.
'Oh, Alice. Here again, I see.'
Keep it light, Kelly.
She just smiled at that, then,
'Can I get you a drink?'
'Oh, thanks, but I'm here to meet someone actually.' No, I really did not fancy sitting and having a drink with her, no matter how long Beth was likely to be. Actually, I realised I found her a little creepy, though I couldn't exactly put my finger on why. Her smile didn't waver as she said,
'Come and have one with me while you're waiting. I can order it from my phone.'
I had no excuse then, so sat with her, at the only seat available at this particular table – beside her, though I put my bag between us as the nearest thing I had to create a bit of a barrier. I cursed the pub 'variety of seating' policy then – I would much rather have

been at one of the more common tables and sat opposite her, kept my distance. While we waited for my drink to arrive she began with the small talk. At least, what I thought was just small talk.

'You've seen the article then,' as she indicated the Chronicle poking out from the top of my bag.

'Oh, yes, it's marvellous for us,' I replied, deliberately referring to the one about my company. She would have no reason to know where I worked, though, so my attempt at deflection was a bit moot.

'Marvellous?' she said darkly. 'I think it's scurrilous.'

I knew which one she meant, but I wasn't going to allow her to see that it had any effect on me.

'Scurrilous? I don't think we're talking about the same article,' and I laughed thinly.

'Page one and two,' she said, almost between her teeth, and I could see she was barely under control.

'Oh, no, I was talking about the middle spread,' and I pulled the paper out of my bag, opened it to the Bellows article, and laid it on the table in front of us.

Please, Alice, let me deflect you. I don't want to have a conversation with you about Tim or the Guardians.

She immediately grabbed it, and flipped it closed so that the front page was uppermost.

'No, that one!' and she stabbed at the little banner in the corner. 'They're trawling for dirt!'

I didn't know what to say. I certainly wasn't going to give her any reason to associate it with me.

'Oh, I haven't seen that,' I said, disingenuously, but my heart was fluttering as if I had been caught out, and I was sure she could see right through me.

She turned the page so I had no choice but to acknowledge the editorial column. I glanced at it, feigning interest, then said,

'Oh, I'm sure it's not that bad.'

'Somebody's after us, Kelly. You wouldn't know anything about that, would you?'

The fluttering turned into full palpitations, as I scrabbled to find the right words, anything to divert this conversation. I spluttered blandness,

'Me? I left them ages ago. I haven't had anything to do with them.'
My equilibrium was shot, and I no longer knew what I was denying, or what was going to come out of my mouth next. I was more than relieved then, when I saw Beth striding into the garden from the car park and heading towards us. I stood up sharply, and called out to her. I knew she had already seen me, but I didn't care – I just wanted the torture with Alice to stop. I stepped around the end of the table and pulled her into a big hug.

'Beth! You made good time.'
I turned to introduce her to Alice, more to put a full stop to the conversation than out of courtesy, to see Alice hoisting her bag onto her shoulder as she stood up.

'You haven't met my friend Beth, have you?' I said, but Alice just nodded at her and muttered, 'I'll see you, Kelly' at me, and left, heading out of the gate quickly, as if she wanted to get away. Her parting words felt like a threat.

'Blimey,' said Beth as she took the seat Alice had been sitting in, 'who was that? Is she always that rude?'
I guess I had been holding my breath, as I found myself exhaling deeply. I started to tell Beth what had been happening, but she stopped me,

'I want to hear this, but I need a drink. That's a long old trip.'
'I'll get it. I've got the app on my phone,' I said as I reached into my bag. My phone was not there.

I suppose I knew immediately what had happened to it, but that didn't prevent hope from propelling me though an increasingly ridiculous series of hoops: first, I scrabbled through my bag, praying I had put it in a different pocket, then I tipped the whole bag out onto to the table in front of us and waded through the used tissues, old receipts and half-eaten packets of Polo mints, to no avail. Finally, in desperation, I demanded Beth join me in retracing my route from work, scouring the ground, to see if I had dropped it on the way. All the while I knew instinctively that my quest was futile – Alice had taken it, I was certain.

Once we were sure it was lost I dissolved while Beth just hugged me, trying to be soothing and reassuring, but I was beyond being pacified.

'You know what's on it, Beth. They've got it. They've got all the evidence I have.'

'You don't know that. It could just be lost.'

There was no real conviction in her voice. She knew as well as I did that we had lost the battle along with the phone, while my mind was filled with images of Tim and his ghastly cohorts sniggering in triumph as they listened.

Beth insisted on reporting the loss of my mobile, and we phoned the police as soon as she got me home. I could hear they weren't very interested – how many phones were lost or stolen in any given week? And they certainly didn't have the time or resources to chase every one. But they took my details anyway, and I suppose I was added to a list somewhere, maybe just as a statistic. I didn't tell them why it was so important to me. I mean, what would I actually have said? 'I don't want to lose the recording I've got of me being raped.' Or perhaps, 'There's damning evidence on it against our mayor, your boss.' And there were several possible responses to that, none of them favourable to me: they might not believe me, or think I was a crackpot; they would prosecute me for trying to slander somebody important with no evidence; they would take me seriously and go straight to Tim with all his charm, power and plausible deniability. No, I was going to have to suck this one up, though it didn't sit easily.

Of course Beth invited me to come and stay at her place, but I needed my own cocoon again, and sent her off, after she had given me an old mobile she had in her car. That lifted our mood a little, momentarily. I mean, who carries an old phone in their car?

I didn't actually go to bed, but I must have dozed off at some point

because I was woken by the doorbell ringing quite insistently. I checked my watch to find it was after 9 in the morning, and scrambled off the sofa and down the stairs, still in my clothes from yesterday. I was instantly nervous, and wasn't going to open the door to anybody until I was very sure who it was. I called out, 'Who is it?' and was pleasantly surprised when the reply was,
'The police. Could you open the door, please?'
Had they found my phone, or at least taken my report seriously? I flung the door open to find two rather dour-looking people on my doorstep, both holding out ID towards me.
'I'm DI Rachel Howarth,' said the one at the front, handing me her card by way of introduction. She was tall and dark and noticeably pretty, with a smart blazer and jeans on, and she indicated the wiry little chap in a suit behind her, 'and this is Darren Baldwin. May we come in, please?'
Blimey, a DI. That seemed a little high-up to come and talk to me about a lost mobile.
'Is this about my phone?' I asked as I led them up the stairs. They didn't answer at all until we were sitting in the front room. I offered them coffee, which they declined, and waited while Rachel took a notebook and pen out of her bag. She looked me squarely in the eye, and I was suddenly uncomfortable.
'Can you tell me about your relationship with Peter Compton?'
Well, that wasn't what I was expecting to hear.
'Relationship?' I floundered for a moment. 'I wouldn't really call it a relationship at all. Just a professional one.'
'In what way?' she pressed on, either not noticing or not caring that I was now distinctly uneasy. Where was this going? Had he given them my recording?
'Am I in trouble?' I asked.
'For what?' she said, rather more grammatically than I would have expected. (I suppose that indicated my own prejudices, that I didn't expect a police officer to speak so grammatically.) I hated people answering questions with questions, so I tried to play her at her own game and repeated my earlier question.
'Have you not come about my phone, then?'

'What about your phone?' she said. Another question, but she wasn't being disingenuous – she really had no idea what I was talking about.

'I lost it yesterday. Actually, I think it was stolen. I did report it. I thought that's why you were here.'

'No,' she said, 'but that explains why we couldn't reach you on it,' and she nodded at Darren. 'We will look into that.' She meant it – she really was going to 'look into it', and I wondered why.

'Thank you,' I said, aware that I was talking quietly now, in anticipation of I didn't know what.

'Can you tell me about Peter Compton?'

'Pete. He's a reporter for the Chronicle.'

'We know that. We found your name in his diary, several times, and wondered how you knew him.'

I went with the innocent first, hoping that would be enough.

'He came to my company, Bellows, this week. He did a story about us.'

'Yes,' she said, 'we saw that. Nice article,' and there was a hint of a smile for the first time since she had arrived. 'But before that. Did you know him? Did you ever meet socially?'

'Not exactly.' I was being cagey now, and we both knew it.

'But you did meet.' A statement, not a question this time.

I decided to go with the truth then, at least a slimmed-down version of it, and told her about meeting him at the count, the lift home (though not the state I was in), a little of our shared suspicion of Tim Byrne and the Guardians. I didn't go into detail about that. The longer I could hold off from revealing the attack the better, as far as I was concerned, at least until I knew where she stood about Tim. For all I knew, she could be a member of the damned party and he was her hero.

'I suppose we met three or four times in total.'

She nodded then, and I assumed I had confirmed what she already knew.

'How did he seem to you, the last time you met?'

What an odd question.

'He was fine. I think he was proud of the article.'

'And that was the last time you saw him? Or spoke to him.'
I remembered the late call on Thursday.
'He called me on Thursday, just as they were going to press. I think he just wanted me to know his story was all done.'
'And how was he then?'
'Actually, he sounded quite excited. He knew he'd done a good job.'
'He wasn't depressed, as far as you know?'
'Far from it,' I said, as an icy hand crept up my back, and I realised she had referred to Pete in the past tense throughout our conversation.
She looked at Darren then, and I could see her trying to make a decision.
'What's happened?' I said, worried now.
'I'm sorry to tell you that Pete's remains were found at the Moor Street car park early this morning.'
I had no words.

The rest of their visit is a bit of a blur. I think Darren made us all coffee at one point, though neither of them finished theirs before they left. I could see them trying to work out why I was so upset about someone I knew so slightly, and they gave me a few more details, presumably to try and put my mind at rest that I was not under any suspicion. They believe he jumped from the top floor of the multi-storey, depressed because his relationship had broken up recently. I didn't mention that he had actually been quite breezy about that, and I suppose I hoped his ex would tell them so. They had come to see me only because his diary told them I was one of the last people he had spoken to. All I could think of was how vulnerable I was again: with my phone gone, and the nearest thing I had a to a witness dead, I had no shield against the worst Tim could throw at me.

9.

There was no obvious or immediate fallout from Pete's death, though in truth I don't know what I was expecting: the Chronicle printed a really affectionate obituary the following week, but had already replaced him, so they moved on more quickly than I did; I renewed my order for weekly delivery, so I could keep an eye on any follow-up, and resolved to get to his funeral if at all possible – saying goodbye was the least I could do; Pete's campaign to find leverage against Tim and the Guardians died with him; the coroner ruled it as suicide, 'while the balance of his mind was temporarily disturbed', and the circumstances meant it was a few weeks before we could say a proper farewell. While I was waiting, I found myself somehow moving slowly, thinking about him a lot. My initial panic at his death had subsided into a sort of general sadness, and as time went on, I was less and less worried that Tim might have reason to come at me: Pete had clearly respected my need for anonymity.

It was at the memorial service that it all changed.

The intervening weeks had seen a cataclysmic shift in national politics. Following the implosion of the Lib-Dems a few years back, and the inability of any of the fringe parties to fill the void, we were now unequivocally a two-party country. Both of these major parties, however, managed to enter a period of self-destruction at the same time, leaving a frightening vacuum. First, the Labour party indulged in some really childish in-fighting (not for the first time) that rendered them fractured and unelectable. Then came the astounding news that made international headlines for weeks – our Prime Minister, who had campaigned on the triple clichés of family values, law and order and immigration controls, was arrested for double bigamy. The arrest was very public, as he left the House after a late-night sitting, and all the media had been informed it was about to happen, I'm sure – they were all there, cameras flashing away, and people with microphones shouting questions at the bewildered and frazzled man at the centre of the melee. All the news media covered it in minute and gloating detail, of course, as befits such a salacious tale. The first wife was a Russian lass he had married when he was a student. It was all arranged through a shady agency, and he hadn't even met her until the day of the wedding. She got spousal citizenship, he got a large sum of money, and they shook hands and parted ways after a nice lunch at a restaurant near the registry office, since when, one might assume, he hadn't given her a second thought. He went on to take a more traditional route, and married a childhood sweetheart when she declared herself pregnant with his baby. He was only just out of university, and didn't love her, just thought he was 'doing the decent thing'. When it transpired, within weeks of the wedding, that she wasn't pregnant at all and had tricked him deliberately, he abandoned her and airbrushed her out of his life altogether. It was this 'wife' who had been the initial whistleblower, mostly for the money that was now being thrown at her from all the news outlets, but also out of late-onset vindictiveness. His current 'wife' was the 'real' one, the mother of his three children, the one who stood by his side smiling inanely at the years of party conferences and election triumphs, and was currently packing her bags to move out of number 10 in fury and humiliation.

The media were all over everything then, and while all the investigations were going on there were a lot of nervous Tories, and a raft of dreadful exposes with far-reaching consequences. The PM had recklessly (arrogantly?) recommended the agency to some of his impoverished student friends as a way to offset their student loans, so a couple more of these fake brides emerged in the lower ranks of the party (though the others had at

least had the decency to divorce them before moving on). One newspaper claimed to have found half a dozen illegitimate and hidden children of various ministers, while another concentrated on the financial consequences of a range of secret accounts that amounted to serial tax-evasion and even money-laundering.
It was a glorious period for anarchists, anti-republicans and detractors of all political shades, who felt themselves vindicated in their cynicism. Meanwhile, those of us of a more circumspect nature worried for the future of our nation. Unsurprisingly, the PM's arrest coincided with a landslide no-confidence vote, a quick date set for a General Election, and campaigning began in earnest within the week.

Thoroughly untroubled, though, were Tim Byrne and his associates all over the country. They had been standing in the wings, waiting for just such an opportunity, and were seizing it with enthusiasm. It wouldn't have surprised me to discover that they were, in fact, behind some of the initial revelations, though I had no idea how they might have engineered that. I had watched with growing unease as politicians tried to distance themselves from the scandal in their own parties, and looked to escape the guilt by association by finding allegiances elsewhere. All over the country people were suddenly 'discovering' the Guardians, with their reputation for moderation and common decency, and their numbers were swelling daily. With their talent for powerful publicity, they found themselves asked for comment on local and national television shows, talking with carefully-rehearsed dignity and balance, getting their names known and their policies heard. They were careful not to be seen as capitalising upon the misfortune of their rivals and colleagues, and refrained from the crowing that was echoing throughout the other parties and the media. Even I could recognise what they appeared to be offering in terms of an alternative to the complacency of the previous regimes, and their sickly strapline was now on everyone's lips until I was weary of hearing it - 'they will look after us'. Not if my own experiences were typical, they wouldn't!

Their most significant coup, however, was getting a national newspaper on their side (though I'm sure they wished it had been the Guardian). The Enquirer (nothing to do with the American gossip-rag of the same name) had been paddling along for generations in the centrist midwater between the great broadsheets and red-tops of the right and left. They were deliberately not aligned with any particular political opinion or philosophy, and had even adopted the 'Berliner' paper size – neither broadsheet nor tabloid - to emphasise their moderate stance in everything, and were viewed with a slightly grudging respect. I had never met anybody who took it as their newspaper of choice; indeed, if I had ever thought about it, I might have wondered how they were still in business. In fact, they almost weren't, which is what allowed Andrew Byrne, Tim's brother, to swoop in to save its life with a hostile and cut-price takeover, thereby giving the party its major mouthpiece, though the world didn't find out about the underhand purchase until much later. The first any of us knew about their radical conversion to political affiliation was when they bought television advertising space to announce their 'Guardian special', and it seemed everybody I knew bought a copy, largely out of curiosity. It was a revelation: the whole paper was devoted to the Guardians. There were photographs and mini-biographies of the main players, with Tim and his friend Russell front and centre as the party founders, a long and entertaining article outlining their history and development from a student pressure-group to a major player, and thumbnail biographies of their members who would be standing in the upcoming election, a significant number of whom were transferees from the fallen parties. Inside the front page was an editorial urging people to vote for them (with the damned strapline prominent!), and the final section was a full reproduction of their manifesto, with notes and summaries ensuring the reader understood how good it all was going to be 'when they are in power'. When, not if. The whole thing was littered with smart quotes and bon-mots from the candidates, but it was the front page headline that I found most terrifying: in huge black letters was, 'VOTE FOR TIM', with the sub-heading, 'they really will look after us all'. I shuddered when I saw it.

This first bumper edition emerged on the day before Pete's memorial. I only glanced at it when I bought my copy at lunchtime, and waited till I was home from work to settle down and concentrate. It was the manifesto I really wanted to scrutinise. Would I find the reality hiding in the rhetoric? Would they show their true colours? Or maybe Tim really was a bad apple, and the rest of them were as decent as they claimed to be, so there would be nothing suspicious for me to unearth. I could only hope.

The manifesto began as an expanded version of the one I had first encountered all those months ago in my own kitchen, with an outline of their predominant philosophy and aims. But this time I was not swept away with the grandiose claims and high expectations. Next came a series of bullet-points listing their main policies, and I suspect most people reading it would have got no further than this handy digest – it was all so plausible, laudable even. It was in the following detail that I found what I was looking for.

First, the environment section was radical and exciting: pour billions into the necessary research to make our country self-sufficient (a worrying concept in itself – where did that leave globalism?) with green energy (wave and wind power), and similarly offer almost bottomless funding to replace fossil-fuel-based consumables with bamboo and hemp 'plastics'. It was unarguably progressive. Next came the finance and business section, and here I could forecast a surging resistance from the erstwhile fat-cats of industry: all salaries, including those of managers, directors, even owners of businesses, must be capped at a specific percentage of all the workers' pay, and no bonuses could be paid without demonstrating the successful completion of rigorous targets. Cats and pigeons sprang to mind, though I was already entertained by anticipating the outcry from the 'haves' at being forced to share their spoils.

The proposal first to raise my concern was in the Home and Society section. The chapter began harmlessly enough – temporary disabled badges for people with injuries or time-limited health conditions (why had nobody thought of this before?), and giving wider responsibilities back to local councils (free recycling and refuse collection to stop fly-tipping, less restraint on building works – though that was couched in terms of 'more freedom' for homeowners). Then came the first pause for thought: each region was to develop its own 'Justice Centre', a huge complex of courts, police stations, forensic laboratories, probation services and so on, all on one site. The theory of these monstrosities was the streamlining of the system, and I was sure they would speed up the whole process as intended, but surely there were compelling reasons for the separation of these bodies, in reducing opportunities for collusion between agencies, and recognising their competing needs and drivers. However frustrating our cumbersome judicial system could be, that very sluggishness gave all parties time to gather evidence and arguments, and reflect before making decisions, and for the benefit of the system users, surely? I couldn't dislodge the notion of 'police state' from the back of my mind. It reminded me of the 'superschool' policy in the first manifesto, and sat no more comfortably.

I then found the hair standing up on the back of my neck when I discovered a commitment to reduce teenage pregnancies and help childless couples, which sounded reasonable on first reading, but was alarming in the juxtaposition of the two groups. It was carefully drafted to sound like a positive step, using terms like 'appropriate support' and 'targeted funding', but what was barely concealed under the rhetoric was the unmistakeable idea that one would solve the other – these people who were promising to 'look after us' were actually proposing that any girl having a baby without being able to demonstrate how she would support it by herself would lose it to a childless couple who could. These already vulnerable girls would be denied benefits, housing, support; even maternity provision would be limited until the family they would 'donate' their baby to was identified and legally contracted. It made no allowance for families who were prepared to look after their single mothers, made no reference to the futures of the displaced children, and suggested no responsibility from the men and boys involved. It was terrifying, and my highly visual imagination was conjuring ghastly scenes of our newly-established police state overseeing babies being dragged from the arms of their young mothers while their self-satisfied boyfriends looked on from a distance. I read and reread this section, to see if I had missed something vital, something that would make it a reasonable proposal after all, but it was clear – this was a modern Lebensborn, nasty social engineering at its worst. I wondered what they would propose next. Selective breeding? Eugenics?

Then, most frightening of all, right at the end of the document was a quite short section entitled 'Controlling press excess', the very title a value judgement. It was proposing to limit press freedom and made the assumption that all journalists were leeches with no sense of decency, and who intruded into people's lives. I have always been opposed to any curbing of the press – they should be allowed to print anything that is true, as long as there is easy access to the means to sue when something is untrue. Without a free press who would hold a mirror up to corporate corruption? Who would call our rulers to account? Who would root for the Davids against the Goliaths? The recent round of government resignations gave me all the proof I needed that they must be allowed to investigate everything and anything on behalf of the rest of us – it was a national newspaper that had first discovered the prime minister's sleazy past. I had some idea why Tim and his chums would seek to silence their public detractors, and all I could think of was Pete.

I had found what I hoped might be their Achilles' Heel – surely no one in their right mind could possibly endorse this proposal, and I can't have been the only one to spot it hiding in plain sight - but I saw no comment anywhere, despite the media being full of this new newspaper and its contents. Perhaps the general feeling was that these policies, each of which affected only a small proportion of the electorate after all, were a price worth paying for the rest of the Guardians' refreshing agenda. I knew I couldn't just cross my fingers and hope it would work itself out, but I had even less idea what I was going to do with the knowledge of my discoveries, which were, after all, hiding in plain sight.

It was at the memorial service that the opportunity presented itself. Dressed smartly in respectful black, though drawing the line at wearing a hat and veil, I took my place among the mourners in the back rows of the large meeting room, and looked around me. Before I sat down and obscured my own view of the proceedings, I took in some of the main players down at the front. The people I imagined to be Pete's family were highly visible by their open grief, and I could feel only sadness for their terrible loss. I was sure they would be reproaching themselves in the way everybody does when somebody close kills themselves, especially one so young and apparently contented: they would be wondering if they might have spotted the signs, maybe even have prevented the whole thing. With them was an almost inconsolable young man in a long black leather coat and gloves, and I speculated that this was Pete's boyfriend. My heart broke for him – how much responsibility did he believe he carried for what had happened? Immediately behind the family, and looking suitably sympathetic, I noted DC Darren Baldwin, there as part of the family liaison service, I presumed.

Before I went I hadn't given any thought to who else might be there, and it was with a little shock that I noticed a strong turnout of our local dignitaries on the other side of the central aisle from the family. Of course they were going to be there! They filled two rows, and were led, naturally, by Tim Byrne himself, our esteemed mayor. The fragrant Shannon, now his wife, was with him, and I saw Alice, Audrey, John and Ashraf, and many of the rest of our Council, even Chandni Patel. I shouldn't have been shocked, of course – he will have written about them all at some point. More shocking, however, was the callousness of having a very visible photographer recording the rehearsed sombreness of the political group, presumably for publication later – the caring party publicly mourning their loss and making sure the rest of the world knew it.

The unmistakeable beauty and thoughtfulness of the service, photographer notwithstanding, was mitigated by the awful vocalisations of grief from the front row, which became almost contagious: everyone in the room was crying openly or trying to stifle their sobs before we were even halfway through the proceedings. It began with a biography of this clever and ambitious young man, his stellar educational career and extensive list of hobbies (he flew gliders and baked his own bread – what a combination!); this was followed by several readings from the family, who all spoke about him with real love, as a man of energy, integrity and decency, and a seeker after truth – hence his chosen profession - and I found myself nodding along – yes, he was a good man. The final piece was the one which finished us all off: a stuttering reading by Martin, the shattered boyfriend I had identified earlier, was billed as Pete's favourite poem, and I could see why. 'Secrets' by the little-known Lola Ridge talked about wounds and disintegrating dreams and ended with an image of the 'bloody foot-prints' left by secrets. In the circumstances of his death, it was poignant beyond belief, and when Andrea Bocelli's soaring tenor closed the event with 'Time to Say Goodbye' nobody moved towards the door. In the end Tim was the first to break the mood of despair, by turning out of his seat and leading the political group up the centre of the room towards the big double doors at the back. I was appalled at his insensitivity: not only did he not allow the family to lead the little procession as was traditional, but he seemed to be trying to make political capital out of the occasion. He nodded and smiled at faces he recognised as he passed, and even managed a couple of brief handshakes on his way through, all, of course, recorded by the photographer, who walked backwards in front of him like a paparazzo at a society wedding.

Until he passed me. I couldn't help myself and muttered 'You're a disgrace,' as he came level with the row I was in. I really didn't mean for him to hear it, didn't even mean to say it out loud, but he stopped, the smile rictus-fixed, and said,
'Kelly, long time no see. How good of you to come.' Like it was an event he was hosting! 'Don't go without saying hello, eh?' An instruction.
It was truly chilling, and I felt as threatened at that moment as I had at any time since I had known him.

While the rest of the company filed out, with me, of course, almost last because of where I was sitting, I had determined to slip away without him catching me. I knew there was no chance of that as soon as I stepped out into the wan sunlight – he was right beside the door, waiting for me. I immediately put my head down and tried to keep walking, but his hand was on my arm before I could break stride, and it was no gentle touch - the grip was actually hurting me. I could not have broken away without making a scene, and, despite all that had gone on between us, I was still too British and reserved to draw attention to myself at such a difficult moment for other people. The rest of his party were already spread through the crowd, making small-talk, offering condolences (though how sincere they were I could only guess), and just Shannon was left beside him. He dismissed her with a nod and a firm, 'I'll catch up with you', and she scuttled off to join one of the other groups. I couldn't tell if she was as cowed by him as I was, but she certainly complied without question.

For the first time since I had met him, the smile wavered, as he turned towards me so his face couldn't be seen by anybody else. Wow – had I really got under his skin that much? He wasted no time with niceties and snarled at me,

'What are you doing here?'

As if I had no right to be here!

'It's a public event,' I tried to assert myself. 'I wanted to say goodbye, like everybody else.'

'You're not welcome,' he said, his grip on my arm digging in even more tightly, until I was sure I would have bruises to show later.

Just for a moment I managed to dredge up some resistance,

'That's not your decision, is it?'

'Not now, maybe,' and the smile was back. 'Let's see in a few weeks, shall we?'

'What, you're going to issue lists of approved mourners at funerals, are you?'

'It's amazing what you can achieve when you're in charge,' he said, and I knew he meant 'in charge of the country'.

I laughed nervously, and said, in a very insulting mock-German accent,

'We haf vays of making you talk, is that it?'

'Or maybe we have ways of making you *not* talk.'

He leaned forward then, until his nose was barely six inches from mine, and that intense gaze was focussed on my eyes.

'You have nothing to talk to anybody about, do you, Kelly?'

The last tiny slip of resistance gone, I just shook my head.

'That's what I like to hear. Good girl.'

Being patronised by this odious bully felt like another form of assault. Then, just as he had beaten me again, he blew it all for the sake of one last cheap shot, 'You're not recording this on your phone as well, are you?' said with a snide little grin.

And then I knew that my previous suspicions were well founded – it was Tim's lap-dog Alice who had taken my phone that evening at the Beggars' Arms, and on Tim's orders, I was sure. The sequence slotted into place like coins into a slot machine: why did Alice take my phone? Because of the incriminating recording on it. How did she know about the recording on my phone? From Tim. But how did Tim know about it? It could only be from Pete, crusader Pete. Had he thought to confront Tim with my graphic accusations, despite his promise to me? And the last coin dropped: nobody had ever found Pete's phone after he died. This was written off as strange but not unheard of – he had probably tossed it into the river on his way to the car park. But now I knew differently, and I was as certain as if I had seen it myself – Pete didn't jump.

I looked up into those blazing eyes, and held his gaze as he had held mine.
'It was you, wasn't it?'
Again, he didn't flicker. This man was steel inside.
'My phone. It was you.'
'I'm sure I have no idea what you mean,' and this time the expression was unmistakeable – he was playing with me.
'And Pete,' I said, and I felt my bottom lip quiver. 'It was you.'
He lifted my arm sharply and jammed it against the frame of the big doors just behind me, wrenching my shoulder into an unnatural position. I thought he was going to break it. I don't know if it was arrogance from knowing that he was getting away with it, or just to reinforce the threat to me, but he denied nothing.
'Well, just make sure it isn't you next time, eh?'

10.

I knew I no longer had a choice about keeping secrets. This man was truly dangerous, and should never be allowed to hold office of any kind again, local or national. Now I just had to hope I could summon enough evidence to make sure he didn't, though it felt like me against the world. As soon as I got home I rummaged on the hall-table and found the business card DI Rachel Howarth had given me – the hell with keeping this quiet; look where that had got me last time. I rang her and left a voicemail, explaining who I was and letting her know I had something important to tell her. Next I rang Beth, who was on her way back from her current project in Portsmouth. I didn't want to break her concentration from driving by talking for any length of time, but I briefly outlined my meeting with Tim at the memorial, and told her I had left a message for Rachel Howarth. She put the two items together with little help from me, and her appetite for the dramatic was whetted. She estimated she could be with me before seven, which gave me an idea of when I could arrange to talk to Rachel – I had no intention of doing it alone.

Rachel rang back within the hour and it was a slightly strained and awkward little conversation. I gave her no details beyond those I had left on the voicemail, just that I had something important to tell her about Pete's death.

'Can you make an appointment to come into the station?' Standard procedure, I assumed, and she was perfectly friendly.

'I'm sorry, I don't want to do that,' and I knew I sounded pathetic, possibly even a little unhinged.

'It's how things are done, Ms Arben,' she said, and I could hear the tone stiffening.

I took a deep breath.

'I think it would put me at risk to be seen coming to see you. Please can you come to me? It's urgent.'

There was a long pause, and I think she was weighing up just how mad I was. Finally, she must have decided she could handle this small paranoid lunatic and agreed, to my relief.

'I can pass you on my way home. Would about eight o'clock be convenient?'

Perfect.

She arrived only about twenty minutes after Beth, and I think she was surprised to find I wasn't alone.

'Ms – ?' she asked a little pointedly.

'Jeffs,' said Beth warmly, shaking her hand, 'but it's Beth. I'm just the critical friend here,' and there was an immediate thawing between them.

She took the chair opposite us and opened with the neutral,

'Now how can I help you?'

I glanced at Beth for support, and began my unlikely tale with what I hoped would be a disarming,

'I know you're going to think me mad, but I don't think Pete Compton's death was suicide. It wasn't even an accident.'

She didn't speak, just blinked at me, so I continued, trying not to overdramatise what I had to say.

'I think he was pushed or thrown off the car park roof.'

'And who do you think might have done that?' She was well and truly suspicious now.

I looked at Beth again, and she nodded – go on.

'Please hear me out,' I was so afraid she would get up and leave, 'but I think it was Tim Byrne, the Mayor. Or his henchmen at least.'

'Henchmen?' she said incredulously.

I couldn't believe my use of the archaic word was the bit she was challenging.

'And what makes you think that?' She was still wary.

Now I had finally started I couldn't stop, as the ghastly sequence of events poured out of me like a nasty dose of vomiting, and I became more and more animated and upset as the memories assumed clarity in the narrative. I swallowed my embarrassment to tell her about the beginnings of my relationship with Tim, then moved on to the attacks (I even used the word 'rape', which I had found so difficult before), and I described them in some detail to make sure she had a clear picture of the damage he had caused me. Yet again, I was grateful that Beth was my friend, as she took my hand to lend me the strength to get me though this bit. I talked about the recording I had sent to Pete, and my suspicion, more an assumption now, that Alice had taken the phone, and referred to Beth as the closest thing I had to a witness to that. I mentioned what I had found buried in the manifesto as evidence of his nastiness, and finished with our dreadful conversation at the memorial, which was still so fresh in my mind. I even showed her the still-developing finger-shaped bruises on my arm.
'I know they prove nothing – I could have got them from anywhere – but they might give you an idea of just what a bully this man is.'
Rachel listened to all this without interruption, but I could see her leaning forward slightly, eyebrows raised, when I gave her, word for word, the threat implicit in his last words to me – 'just make sure it isn't you next time'.

'That's quite a tale, Ms Arben.'
I could see her trying to work out what to do with all this information. As I saw it she had three options: laugh at me and leave with a warning not to slander or harass Mr Byrne again; persuade me I was delusional and urge me to seek help for my paranoia; believe me and set up an urgent investigation. I couldn't tell from her very professional approach which option she was going to plump for, but she began gently,
'I assume you have no actual evidence for any of this beyond your own testimony.'
'It was all on my phone.' I was trying to regain my composure,

desperate for her to believe me.
She turned to Beth,
'Did you hear this recording?'
'No,' Beth replied with a mock-weary sigh. 'The idiot woman was too embarrassed to play it to me.'
Rachel gave a little chuckle at the use of the word 'idiot' from a friend, and I was happy to note their burgeoning collusion.
'But she did tell you about it?'
'Much later, yes, once she was over being embarrassed.'
'Did you tell anybody else about any of this?' This to me.
'Just Pete Compton. And look what they did to him.'
'We don't know that for certain.'
I was immediately relieved – although she wasn't seizing my story as gospel, she wasn't completely dismissing it either.
'But you never found his phone. Isn't that suspicious in itself?'
'Sadly, no,' she shook her head. 'It's only in the movies that people leave suicide notes and clues.'
'What about his computer? Didn't he leave notes about what he was working on? Did you check with the Chronicle?'
There had to be something somewhere. Surely, in his determination to 'bring Tim down' as he had told me, he wouldn't have relied on memory alone.
Rachel paused then, and I could tell she was trying to make a decision.
'Look, I really shouldn't tell you this, and I'm not going to go into detail, but we did find a memory-stick in his desk at the Chronicle.'
I was instantly excited.
'What? About Tim?'
'Let's just say he had been collecting information. It was a very disorganised set of rough notes. Snippets. Cagey and coded. And only he would have known what the codes meant.'
'Did he mention me?' Now I was almost wishing I hadn't made him swear to keep me anonymous.
'Only in passing. Just your name, really.'
I had the distinct impression that she would be going back to this little find to try and make sense of it, but she wouldn't tell

us anything more about it for now. She finished the interview by taking some details about dates and times, presumably as an initial check on Tim's movements. It made sense – if he was abroad or somewhere distant at a time when I was claiming he was here with me, then the whole story would collapse. But I was confident – now he was a public figure he couldn't hide, and his appearances were well-documented.

She left us with the standard,
'I'll be in touch.' Then, as she shook both our hands at the front door,
'I can see why you might believe yourself to be at risk.'
I felt more than relief. Though she wasn't yet totally convinced, I had at least been heard.

It was two nights later that things became really scary. Just as I was getting up to go off to bed I heard that sound, the one that had so frightened me in the past – the key in the door. I stood on the landing looking down at the front door, instantly frozen, trying to become small and silent. The logic of the changed lock didn't matter – he was trying to get to me again. The key clicked twice, three times, then was pulled out of the lock, useless. I listened intently, hoping to hear retreating footsteps, but jumped when instead there began a pounding on the door. Three big thumps, then a man's voice I didn't recognise,
'Open this door! I know you're in there.' It wasn't Tim. One of his 'henchmen', I assumed.
Two more thumps, lower down the door this time – these were kicks.
'Open the door, Kelly!'
Not a chance. I just had to hope the door would hold.
While the banging and shouting continued, I managed to free myself from whatever terror had briefly robbed me of movement and went to my bag to grab my phone. Rachel Howarth's number was in the memory and I pressed the green button, hoping she would answer quickly.

'Rachel Howarth.'
I had to hope I could convey the urgency while whispering, but I didn't need to.
'What on earth is that noise?'
'They're trying to get in! Please help me.'
'Phone 999, now,' she said. 'Do it, Kelly. Hang up. Call 999. They'll get there quicker than I can.'
I did as I was told, and the emergency operator told me to stay on the line until rescue arrived. I was glad of the witness, even if she couldn't actually see what was happening to me. With her listening in, I yelled frantically down the stairs to my unseen attacker beyond the door,
'I've called the police. They'll be here any second,' and the noise from the front door stopped as suddenly as it had begun. I should have felt relieved, but the silence was eerie, unnerving. I heard the operator in my ear,
'Are you still there?'
'Yes, I'm still here. It's all gone quiet.'
'Don't worry, they're still on their way. Just another couple of minutes.'
But before she had finished speaking I heard and saw the letterbox moving, as something white and heavy dropped through onto the hall carpet. I had no time to wonder what it was as it burst into a sheet of flame, immediately obscuring the lower half of the door, and spreading as quickly across the width of the little entranceway.
'Oh, my god,' I yelled into the phone. 'It's on fire.'
The operator was still the essence of calm.
'Can you put it out without hurting yourself?'
Yes, yes, I could pour something on it, and I ran to the kitchen. Though I wasn't rational enough to think of it at the time, I was glad of my mother's domestic advice – in the sink was a plastic washing-up bowl full of the soapy water I had used to wash up after dinner earlier, 'ready for the supper things, dear'. I dropped the phone and grabbed the bowl with both hands, then ran back to the landing and flung the water down the stairs and onto the fire.

This time there was relief as the flames died in a hiss of steam. At the same moment I heard sirens, not so distant, and knew I was going to be safe.

Everything slowed down for a bit then. I walked back to the kitchen and replaced the bowl in the sink, then picked up my phone from the surface where it had fallen. As I did so, I could hear the tinny little voice,
'Are you still there?'
'Yes, it's alright,' and I was a little breathless. 'I've put it out.'
'Well done. Can you hear the police? Are they there now?'
As she spoke there was a single knock on the door, and I looked down to see the unmistakeable glow of twirling blue lights through the frosted panel of the door.
'Yes, they're here.'
'Don't hang up until we know it's them. Can you get to the door?'
I ran down the stairs two at a time and wrenched the door open to see a pair of uniformed officers, the open doors of their car gaping behind them.
'Was it you who called, madam?' said one of them, and I must have looked a sight, a frantic woman in slippers, standing in the steaming wreckage of her own hallway.

The formalities were brief, and considerably simplified by the arrival of Rachel a mere ten minutes behind the other two. This meant I didn't have to go over any of the background, or my suspicions, and she dismissed them as soon as they had logged my details and given me a crime number. Once they had gone I made us both coffee – I needed the caffeine hit even if she didn't – and we sat on opposite sides of the room as we had before, blinking at each other. I could hardly hold my coffee as my hands were shaking so much, and the tears came then, readily and plentifully.
'I'm sorry I'm such a mess,' I said, trying to control my emotions.
'Not at all,' she answered warmly, handing me a tissue from her coat pocket. 'Cry away. You need it after that.'
She wasn't wrong. The adrenaline of the last few terrifying

minutes had left me shattered.

Once I had settled enough to hold a conversation, she became the business-like senior officer she had been when we met first.
'Right. We have to decide what we do next.'
'I've no idea. I mean, why did this happen? What did they think they were doing?'
'They were trying to scare you. That's all.'
'Well, they've succeeded,' and the tears were seeping back.
'First, though, I need to be honest with you, Kelly. And I'm sorry, but I think I may bear some responsibility here,' she said disarmingly.
'How?' And I saw it in an instant. 'Please tell me you didn't tell Tim we spoke.'
She paused just long enough to let me know that that was indeed what had happened.
'I wasn't intending to be so direct, but I did need to confirm what I could of your story.'
Why did everybody pass on my confidences? Could nobody keep a secret? Though while I was being so self-centred, I knew that was the only way he was ever going to be stopped – we had to make it all public. I just wished it didn't all have to come at such risk to me.
'Before you get cross with me, let me tell you I met him by accident. Yesterday evening was the annual Mayor's Gala Dinner.'
I knew that to be true – I had seen it in the Chronicle.
'I don't have any choice but to go, every year. My governor hates these do's and makes me go to represent the local force. I was seated way at the back of the hall, with his lordship up on the top table, so it didn't occur to me to say anything to him. But he was doing his usual - circulating, glad-handing, being his charming Teflon self.'
The language she was using told me that she could see through him as clearly as Pete had. But if millions across the country were learning to love him, who's to say which of us is right? He really was Marmite.

'He finally got to our table, just as I was thinking of going home. As it was his gala it would have been rude of me to leave then, so I thought I'd take the opportunity to do a little fishing.'
'And that's when you asked him about me.' I was trying not to be angry with her.
'No, not directly. That's what makes tonight all the more worrying. I just said I'd met a friend of his recently.'
'Me.'
'Yes, you. And I did give him your name. But that was all. No details of your complaints, no accusations, not a hint of what you told me about him and his henchmen.' (See, I wasn't the only one who liked the word.)
'And what did he say?'
'Well, that's what was so odd. When I said you were also a friend of Pete Compton's, he went straight into a very defensive little rant about groupies, and deluded women flinging themselves at him.'
'How dare he?' I could feel my hackles rising.
'I know, I know,' Rachel was moving me on before I could wind myself up.
'I asked him if he meant you directly, were you one of those women, and that's when he slipped up. You've got under his skin, Kelly.'
I wasn't sure whether to be flattered or even more afraid.
'What did he say?'
Her answer was chilling, to say the least.
'Do you remember what he said to you at the memorial?'
How could I forget?
'Let me see if I can remember his exact words.'
I knew she was playing with me now, for dramatic effect, I suppose – she remembered exactly what he said.
'She needs to make sure she's not the next one to go off the car park roof.'

The rest of our brief evening was spent on practical matters, beginning with my immediate safety.
'Do you have somewhere you can stay? You'll need to get that door

fixed.'

Not to mention a new hall carpet.

'Could you go and stay with your parents?'

I could, of course, but there were too many objections – not only would it be difficult to get to work from there, but I really didn't want my poor mum and dad to be involved in all this. They would be so worried for me.

'How about Beth's? I offered.

Her answer surprised me.

'Does Tim Byrne know her? Does he know where she lives?'

'No,' I answered cagily. 'Why does that matter?'

'Well, I still have a lot of digging to do, and I don't know how much of your story we'll be able to prove, but I think tonight has shown us that you were right to be concerned about your own safety. I'd feel happier if you were somewhere they don't know about.'

'Yes, I'll go to Beth's. I have a key – we're open house for each other.'

'Good. Can you call her this late to arrange it?'

'No problem,' I said. Beth would actually be furious with me if I didn't tell her straight away what had happened.

I rang her while Rachel washed up our cups and checked that my front door was safe enough for now. I didn't want to go into too much detail, again for both our sakes, but promised to catch her up when she came back at the weekend, and made sure it was ok to go to her place for now.

'Great,' she said lightly, 'you can look after Elvis. He's been missing me.'

'He's not the only one,' I said.

'Will you be OK till the weekend?'

I knew I would be now I felt Rachel was looking after me, and said so.

She rang off with, 'Stay safe, dear girl.'

Rachel stayed while I packed a bag and locked up as best I could, and then followed my car all the way to Beth's. We then danced a sort of reverse of the sequence from when we left my flat - she checked locks and windows, while I unpacked the few things I had

grabbed. I must say I felt safer here than in my own place. First, there was proper security to even get into the building, with state-of-the-art video doorbells, a key-operated lift, and strong double-locked front door. We were also on the third floor, too high up for anybody to get in from the outside. Before she left for the night Rachel reeled off a worrying list of precautions she thought I should take for a while: don't exit any building (work or home) without checking I wasn't being watched; vary my route to and from work; stay with other people as much as possible; don't open the front door unless I knew who was on the other side.
'And call me any time you feel the need.'
I wondered if this was what witness protection felt like!

When I woke the next morning I was disorientated for a moment until the events of last night came back to me in a rush. I felt a mixture of anxiety at the thought of what might have happened and reassurance that Rachel was clearly on my team now. I had time before I had to leave for work, and decided to use it to reflect on recent events. Where had my ordered little life gone? I knew I had started it all when I moved Geoff on, so maybe I had to take responsibility for all that had happened since. I took my coffee out onto the large balcony and sat looking out over the park in the morning sunshine. It really was quite lovely up here, a good place to sit and think. The balcony was big enough to accommodate a small table and a pair of chairs, and Beth and I had sat here often in the past, reading newspapers, putting the world to rights and drinking, so it all felt comfortable and familiar to be here now. The view over the park was calming in itself, and unobscured from wherever I sat – the architects had cleverly designed the front wall from toughened glass, so I felt sort of surrounded by nature. Directly below me the service road was concealed by thoughtfully planted trees and I could almost imagine myself in those very tree-tops. This was the nearest I was going to get to peace for now.

My little reverie was broken by the terrifying sound of a key in the front door, and I jumped to my feet, instantly afraid. I almost cried with relief when I saw it was only Holly, Elvis's minder.

'I'm so sorry, Kelly,' she said, seeing my shock, 'I didn't know you were here.'

Holly was a poppet. She was 15, bright, beautiful and carefree, and lived in the flat below Beth's with her mum, who worked as a nurse at the local clinic. Beth had quickly become friends with both of them when she had moved in here, and for the last couple of years had employed Holly to look after Elvis when she was away. The arrangement worked well for all of them: Holly earned generous pocket money and Beth knew he was being well looked after. Holly's mum was a proper 'mumsy' mum, with an apparent mission to feed everybody, and often sent plates of delicious traditional Caribbean food up with Holly, to feed 'that skinny woman upstairs'. (Let's hope she was still doing it – I could eat well while I was here.) Holly fed Elvis whenever Beth wasn't there, and walked him twice a day, once before she went to school, and again in the evening, and often 'kidnapped' him and took him down to her flat for company when her mum was working long hours. And Elvis was pleased to see her now, running across the room to meet her, wagging his stump of a tail.

'It's OK, Holly,' I pulled myself together quickly. 'You weren't to know.'

'Do you want me to leave him for now?' she offered, but I couldn't disappoint the happy little chap.

'No, take him. Look at him – he can't wait.'

'If you're sure.'

'Pretend I'm not here,' I said, and I wasn't being generous – I didn't want to have to think about dog-sitting on top of everything else. Besides, I'd never been a fan of the commitment that came with pets, and it was good to know someone else would take responsibility for the feeding, exercising and training that came with living with this energetic little guy. Even the multi-tasking specialist Beth needed help, so I knew I wouldn't have stood a chance. He probably wouldn't even survive if it were left to me!

Holly took me at my word and went off with Elvis on his lead, calling out to me as she left,
'See you later.' She would be back for the second walk, I knew.

I managed to get myself out and off to work – there was nothing to be gained from staying here all day on my own, and I needed the distraction and comfort of my usual schedule. It was a very normal day at Bellow's, satisfyingly busy as always, which meant I didn't have time to share what had happened with anybody there, even if I had wanted to. I had learned from the last time during the election to mask my preoccupation with effort, and left at the end of the day with nobody any the wiser about what was happening to me. I did as Rachel had instructed, and had a good look around outside before heading for my car at the end of the day. I even found myself checking my mirror for anybody following me all the way back to Beth's, as if my life were a Bond movie or something. That was ridiculous on several levels, I knew – who would be following me? Would I recognise it if they were? I knew I was being melodramatic, and was glad there was no one to witness it.

When I got back Holly was there, playing with Elvis and a chew-toy, having just fed him, and I found myself inexplicably happy to find the flat occupied. Apart from the fact that this was a delightful little scene in its own right, I realised at that moment that, all the drama notwithstanding, I had missed the company that comes from living with somebody else – it was very pleasant to come home to a place that was lived in even when I wasn't there; perhaps that was the draw for Beth in having an Elvis. Maybe I should see if Geoff wanted to come back. And I laughed inwardly at the very thought – not only had that ship long sailed between us, but he seemed really happy with the lovely Ali. I wasn't serious, but it did make me think about my future, just a little.

As I tossed my coat and bag onto the sofa, (no compulsion to keep it tidy for now, eh?) Holly and I exchanged pleasantries and she got ready to leave after a few minutes.

'Do you want me to take Elvis downstairs?' she said breezily, and I found I didn't really care one way or the other. I said so,

'Up to you. Whatever you like.'

'OK,' she said, 'I'll check if mum's back.'

The loose arrangement worked well. Holly's mum didn't mind how often she brought Elvis home with her, or for how long, but preferred not to have him around when she was cooking – lovely though he was, he was no less a thief than any other dog, given half a chance - or planning a quiet evening in with her daughter. And now he had been fed and walked I didn't mind either way: while I didn't actually crave time with any dog, spending an evening with the very cute Elvis was no trial once his basic needs had been met. So she left him with me, for now at least.

I didn't quite know what to do with myself – living in someone else's home never has the same compulsion to clean or reorganise that it might in your own. I thought about dinner, but made no decision. I pulled up my latest thriller on my kindle, but didn't need any more thrills right now, so put it away again as soon as I had opened it. I flicked on the television, but there were no Premiership matches on tonight and I knew I wouldn't be able to settle to a film or comedy, so turned it straight off again. I wandered around the flat, idly checking the titles on the bookshelf, looking over the cd selection, and finally settled on no decision as my decision – I switched on the radio to be greeted with some bland classic pop as undemanding background noise, then made a cup of coffee and wandered out to the balcony again. It really was one of my favourite places to be, and I sat looking out over the park, trying to empty my mind. If any place could achieve that for me, it was here. I could see people wandering, some striding, through the well-kept grass and along paths; there were dog-walkers (Holly often took Elvis there, I knew) and sitters - people resting on benches; at almost the furthest point I could just make out a couple picnicking on the grass, while on the bench closest to me was a balding, scruffy chap in jeans behind a newspaper. I watched approvingly as he stood and tossed it into a nearby bin before making his way to the gate – well done, no littering in our park. This was a well-used and loved open space, and we'd like to keep it that way.

I closed my eyes and concentrated on my breathing, counting in for 7, holding for 4, out for 12, as my version of meditation. It had worked for me when I had been having trouble getting to sleep in the past, and I was just thinking how nice it would be to drop off here and snooze for a while. I had nearly succeeded when I heard a sharp rap on the front door. That broke the mood and I was instantly a little irritated – why did the child not bring her key? I tutted and made my way steadily to the door, leaving my coffee on the balcony table. But when I wrenched open the door, ready to remonstrate with Holly for not letting herself in, I was horrified to find John Placide filling the doorframe, looking for all the world like a salesman in smart suit and overcoat, and grinning as if in triumph that he had found me. And all I could think was 'henchman'.

'So here you are,' he said, and in other circumstances this would have been a perfectly pleasant and appropriate greeting. But not now.
I thought I had done such a good job of concealing myself, staying alert, keeping myself safe, and I had failed at the first hurdle – why on earth did I open the door without checking who was beyond it as Rachel had told me to? It didn't matter that I thought it was Holly – I should have checked!
'How did you find me?' I spluttered.
'Why? Were you hiding?'
I didn't know how to reply, and knew there was no right answer. I was in trouble here. My mind was racing, trying to grab something useful, something that would extricate me from the threat I now felt as keenly as when somebody had tried to set fire

to my flat. I grabbed the front door to slam it shut, but he was ready for that, and put out a giant paw, stopping the door before it moved more than a couple of inches.

'That's not nice, Kelly. Aren't you going to invite us in?'

Us? It was only then that I noticed he wasn't alone. From behind him emerged a short, sandy little man in his forties, and he was smiling the shark-smile as well. I think I had seen him before (was it the man with the newspaper from the bench?), though I couldn't place him now, and I certainly didn't know his name. It didn't help at all when John introduced him, as if we were at a cocktail party or something,

'Have you met Alan?' as Alan reached around John and offered me his hand to shake. I ignored it. Everything about this encounter was surreal, but I was still prepared to clutch at anything, and John's apparent courtesy gave me a sliver of hope that I could still get away with this.

'No, John, I'm sorry. I'd like you to leave.'

The smiles didn't waver, and I knew then that I was in more danger than ever – they had been taking lessons in arrogance from Tim.

'Sorry, Kelly, can't do that,' and he pushed his way in, forcing me back into the living-room and leaving Alan to close the front door behind him.

First, I tried my go-to strategy - reason.

'I don't know why you're here, John, but I have nothing to give you. I'd like you to go.'

'You said that already,' he was still grinning. 'And yet we're still here.'

Then Alan chimed in,

'And I think you know why we're here.'

I tried a bit of bravado next.

'I have no idea. So tell me. What do you want?'

John just shrugged then, and left it to Alan to intimidate me.

'You've been talking to the wrong people, haven't you?' he said, and his smile dropped for the first time.

And there I was, already resorting to begging,

'I've haven't spoken to anybody. I don't know what you mean. Please.'

Alan continued, 'You've been telling tales.'

How did they know? Had somebody passed on my accusations? Or was this a case of them putting two and two together and coming up with a much bigger number again?

'I haven't spoken to anybody.' I was repeating myself now. 'And told them what? What would I have to tell?'

Then John's smile was gone, too.

'That's what we want to know. And you're going to tell us.' He stepped towards me in deliberate threat, and I knew he wasn't going to be put off.

Alan joined in, 'And you know what happens to people who talk to the wrong people, don't you?'

I thought I knew where this was going now and before I could stop myself I blurted out, 'Pete!'

'Ah,' said Alan, 'Your friend Mr Compton. Such a shame what happened to him.'

'It was you, wasn't it? You pushed him off that roof.'

Shut up, Kelly! Don't make them angry. But they didn't appear to be angry, far from it. John's smile was back in full as he said,

'You'll never know, my dear,' leaving me in no doubt. 'Although you might be finding out how it feels. And sooner than you think.'

My fears were confirmed: they were here to make me 'have an accident'. With nothing to lose now, all I could think to do was try to stall them. Maybe I could hold them off for long enough for Holly to come back for Elvis and rescue me.

'I suppose Tim sent you.'

'Now why would you think that? Is it Tim you've been telling tales about?' Alan's turn.

'I haven't been telling tales. What tales? I have nothing to tell.' I was almost shouting now, but I didn't care – in fact I'd have been delighted if somebody heard me.

'So you're not going to tell us, then.' This was John now – they were a proper double-act, taking it in turns to ask me stupid questions I couldn't answer.

Then Alan gave me a clue. 'Where's your phone?'

So I was right - they had known about the recording. I would have preferred them not to find it, at least not straight away – a search would give me more of the time I was now desperate for, but I couldn't help a glance at my bag, which was sitting on the sofa. Alan saw the look, grabbed my bag and tipped it upside down on the sofa and carpet, finding the phone almost immediately. The most incongruous thoughts appear when we least expect them, and now I was annoyed at the thought that I was going to have to clear up this debris later.

'Let's make sure there's nothing on this one,' he said, and all I could do was watch as he scrolled through whatever he was looking for. I had a small moment of relief as I knew there was nothing incriminating on this phone, but that was shattered when he got to the call log.

'Ooh, look – 999. Now why would you be calling emergency services?'

'I'm sure you know why,' I was getting angry myself now. 'Someone tried to set fire to my flat yesterday. Would you know anything about that?'

Alan just laughed and carried on scrolling. It was when he spoke next that I felt betrayed all over again,

'Hey, John. Here's a number we know.'

He showed the screen to John, who said, almost to himself,

'Ah, the lovely DI Howarth, I believe.'

Of all the numbers there must be within the police system how would they recognise this one? Unless they knew it already. And then I was certain, and more afraid than I had been since the beginning of all this: it was Rachel who had told them what I said and where I was. The very person I had turned to for protection. She had been so plausible.

John took the phone from Alan and put it in his pocket, then turned to me.

'Is that it?' he said, almost sweetly.

I didn't know what sort of answer he expected from me, so I didn't say anything, just shook my head slowly. All I could think of was that I had run out of lifelines now.

'Come on,' he continued. 'Let's go outside,' as Alan led the way onto the balcony.

Everything else is a blur, a hazy mixture of clarity and confusion: I heard screaming and begging from me; I saw my lone little coffee cup on the table as I passed it and heard Abba's 'Waterloo' coming from the radio as if from a distance (surely it should have been Queen's 'Who Wants To Live Forever?', or even Chris Farlowe's 'Out Of Time'); fighting against strong hands on my arms; there was denim and tweed; Elvis yapping and growling; my back hitting the wooden rail on the top of the glass wall; there was sky and greenery.

11.

There is a face. Close to mine. Focus.

There is a voice,
'Hello, darling. Are you in there?'
Mum. Did she die, too? Why didn't I know? Has she been waiting for me?

There are two faces. Close to mine.
A man? Mum. Yes, mum.
'Hello, my love. Can you hear me?'
Yes, mum.

A face. A book.
I can reach out and touch. I can't.

Voices, all distant.

Faces, all close.

Focus. Focus.

Beth.
'She's awake.'
'Hardly,' not Beth.

'Can you hear me, lovey? If you can hear me move your hand.'
Can I?
'She moved it! She can hear me!'
'Shh.'

'I know you're in there. Come on, you malingerer. Buck up.'
I know that voice.
I know all the voices.

A new face.
'Squeeze my hand, pet.'
I squeeze.
"Well done.'

There is no tomorrow, no yesterday, only now, right now. Focus.

Focus. Geoff. Geoff?
'Hi, there.'
'Hi.' My voice. My own voice.
'About time.'
I manage questions, though I'm not sure if I'm registering the answers.
'What time is it?' 'Where am I?'

More focus. Two voices, not close. Two faces, over there. They're chatting, to each other, not to me.
Beth.
'Beth.' Me.
'Yay!'
Close to me now.
'So, where have you been, then, you old hypochondriac?'
'Where am I?'
'Paul Bent Memorial.' Registered.
I see plaster, tubes, bottles.

Finally, a passing of time. I know it's not today.
'What day is it?'
I have discovered that if I speak there is somebody there straight away, somebody to hear me, somebody to answer questions.
'It's Wednesday.'
It's Geoff. Dear old Geoff. And he presses a button.

'So how long have I been here?'
There's a nurse. I've squeezed her hand, I remember.
'This is day 6.' Geoff.
'I've been here for six days?'
'Yes,' the nurse this time. 'You're doing really well.'
'Why are you here?' Me to Geoff.
'We've all done shifts.'
Shifts?

Finally, I have stayed awake long enough to hold a conversation, though it exhausts me. Over the next few days they have been getting longer and longer, and I'm starting to piece it all together.

It was not a good moment when I realised it was Rachel sitting on the other side of the room chatting to Beth. I caught no more than snippets – 'coffee', 'work', some laughter.
'What's she doing here? Don't trust her, Beth. Don't believe her.'
'I thought this was what you'd be thinking. It wasn't me, Kelly.'
'Nobody else knew where I was.'
'It was Alan.'
Alan? Oh, yes, Alan.
'Alan Burton. He's a private investigator, works for the Guardians. He used to be a police officer, worked with me. And he still has friends in the department, with looser lips than mine. Oh, nobody talked to him deliberately, nobody told tales, but when you're in the pub with an old mate, you sometimes forget the rules of confidentiality. Don't worry, they won't be doing that again in a hurry!'
I could see the strategy now, and they were all doing it: throwing information at me in great chunks in the hope some of it would stick before I nodded off again.
'He watched you.'
'But I did what you said. I was careful.'
'Not careful enough, I'm afraid. Not your fault. How could you know?'
So maybe it *was* him on the bench with the newspaper, counting

floors and balconies, tracking me.

There were white coats and blue scrubs, more chunks.
'We sedated you for a while, but you've done well.'
Really? Everything hurts. One arm in plaster. One leg, on the same side. Bruising everywhere else.
'It's about average recovery time for a fractured skull.'
'A what? I fractured my skull?'
'Just a hairline. You'll be fine.'

There was a man in a wheelchair this time, and he looked like a mirror version of me – the other leg and arm in plaster. He was smiling.
'Remember me?
'I think so. Remind me.'
'Darren. Darren Baldwin.'
I was trawling back through the memory banks here. Darren. Darren Baldwin. The DC on my doorstep with Rachel.
'What happened to you?'
'You did.'
This was a chunk of information I really wanted to hear.
'When you came off the balcony I was underneath, and I tried to break your fall.'
'But you broke both of us instead?'
'Not quite. Luckily the trees did a lot of that. But you landed sort of sideways on me. We both went down. The broken bits are where we hit the ground.'
'Just as well I'm little. I could have killed us both.'
'To be honest, there was a time when I thought you had.'

I got to ask Geoff about the shifts.
'I didn't know if you'd remember that conversation.'
'We had a conversation?' Maybe I hadn't lost my sense of humour.
'You've had an army out here, taking it in turns to sit with you, talk to you, be here when you woke up.'
Ah, mum. Beth.

'Beth organised a proper rota. WhatsApp.' Dear, precious Beth. 'Two hour shifts. Even Ali did a couple. She read to you. Remember Ali?'
I knew I liked that woman.
'Who else?'
Your mum and dad, your sister, your brother. Dorette, Rachel. Even Jenna did one. And Holly, and her mum.'
I knew some wonderful people.
'They even wheeled Darren in a few times at night when nobody else could get here.'
Poor Darren, hadn't he suffered enough? Lol.

The army was starting to come in waves now. It was party time in my room. There were a couple of big questions left.
'So how did Darren know to try and catch me? Why was he there?'
There was a bit of mutual glancing, some sniggering. It was Beth who answered.
'With all the time I'm away I wanted to know Elvis was alright. I installed a camera in the flat, an Elvis-cam, if you will, oh, weeks ago. I wasn't hiding it from you, I just hadn't got around to mentioning it. Didn't seem important. And before you ask, it's movement-activated.'
'So you watched it all.'
'It was horrible, I'm not going to pretend. When it came up on my laptop I thought I was going to see Elvis sneaking onto my bed again, and instead I got your own private horror show.'
'Just as well I wasn't dancing naked or bringing back a stream of unsavoury men.'
Everybody laughed at that, even my mum.
'But how did Darren know?'
'I called Rachel as soon as I saw them come in, Alan and what's his name.'
My mind was racing a bit now – the old Kelly was coming back.
'And does this camera of yours have sound?'
'Yep.'
'Does it record?'

'Oh, yes,' Rachel was speaking now, and looking quite pleased with herself. 'We got the lot.'
'So Tim?' The final big question.
'Arrested before night-fall. Him and all his nasty chums. I know it might have looked to you like we weren't doing much, weren't taking you seriously, but we've been investigating since you first spoke to us.'
'So you did believe me, then?'
'Kelly, I always believed you.'
I nearly cried with relief. I wasn't just some mad woman with a political bee in her bonnet.
'What about Pete's notes? Did you ever decipher them?'
'Oh, yes, we got the king of all code-breakers on it. Between that and your testimony, we got pretty much everything we needed. We were almost at the point of making arrests even before we got Beth's call. That just topped it all off. They'll be going nowhere for a very long time.'
'So who did you get?'
'All of them. They're nowhere near as loyal as they'd have you believe. Once we'd pinned down John Placide and Alan Burton, they fell like ninepins. John tried the 'only following orders' trick, and told us in words of one syllable that it was Tim who sent him. Alice tried the same thing with your phone, claimed she didn't know what was on it, but he'd got her vote the same way he got yours, so we knew she had an idea why he wanted it. She's only being charged with theft so far, but I'm certain we'll turn up more when we keep digging.'
'So she still had my phone, then?'
'Worse. She passed it straight to Tim, and the idiot kept it.'
I was fearful again, just for a moment until she put my mind at rest.
'Don't worry, Kelly, it will never be played in public. He has conceded the evidence on it, and it would be much worse for him than you.'
'And are they all charged with the same thing?'
Rachel laughed then. She was enjoying this.

'Let's see. There's murder,' (Pete, I assumed) 'attempted murder,' (that would be me), 'coercion', (half the party, I should think), 'a whole heap of financial impropriety – remember the purchase of the Enquirer?' So they even got Tim's brother.
'And we're not working alone. Did you ever meet his friend Russell? What a nasty piece of work. You think Tim Byrne is sleazy? There are six different police forces across the country with some very unpleasant politicians in their cells right now.
It was mum who spoke this time,
'You brought down a government, sweetheart, before they were even elected.'

ABOUT THE AUTHOR

Allie Byrons

Allie Byrons spent her career in teaching and in the theatre—her two real passions in life. She is now a retired head teacher residing in West London, and has written four novels. Her passions extend beyond theatre and into sport, having contributed numerous articles to a football fanzine. Three decades ago, she lent her expertise to Open University teacher training materials, offering insights into playground dynamics. Throughout her life, writing has been a constant pursuit, whether crafting plays for her amateur dramatics group or penning eulogies for loved ones. Now, with ample time on her hands, she is fully immersed in creating full-length narratives. Her sole literary aspiration is to witness her work in print.

Printed in Great Britain
by Amazon